Beauty on Earth

BEAUTY ON EARTH

By CHARLES FERDINAND RAMUZ

Translated by MICHELLE BAILAT-JONES

Foreword by VALERIE TRUEBLOOD

ONESUCH PRESS

LONDON   MELBOURNE   NASHVILLE

Onesuch Press enriches lives by reclaiming the forgotten past; publishing the lesser known works of great writers and the great works of forgotten ones. For more information about us visit www.onesuchpress.com.

A ONESUCH BOOK
Published by ONESUCH PRESS
PO Box 303BK, Black Hill 3350 Australia

National Library of Australia Cataloguing-in-Publication entry
Author: Ramuz, C.F. (Charles Fedinand), 1878 - 1947.
Title: Beauty on Earth /Charles Ferdinand Ramuz; translated by Michelle Bailat-Jones; introduction by Valerie Trueblood

ISBN: 978 0 9872760-7-0 (pbk.)
ISBN: 978 0 9872760-8-7 (ebook)

Other Authors/Contributors
Bailat-Jones, Michelle, translator.

Dewey Number: 843.912

The paper used in this publication meets the minimum requirements of ANSI/NISO Z39.48-1992 (R1997) (Permanence of Paper). The paper used in this book is from responsibly managed forests. Printed in the United States of America, the United Kingdom and Australia by Lightning Source, Inc.

FOREWORD

"If I have masters, they are among the painters."
Charles-Ferdinand Ramuz

Through the terrace door of a Swiss inn the reader steps into a painting. The figures at the table move: two men, bumbling at first glance, elderly. They could be stagehands in the moments before the actors come on. In an opera they would be the villagers, and in fact, they are the villagers, giving no sign of having any further role to play. There's an awkwardness to the scene; the prose seems to be feeling its way. The paint is still going onto the canvas. The two men talk to each other and before long the writer—someone like them, one of them—begins to address us. Thus commences the fugue that is *La Beauté sur la Terre*, in which the coming of a beautiful orphan to her uncle's inn brings a gradual chaos upon his town.

The great Swiss novelist Charles-Ferdinand Ramuz published *La Beauté* in 1927. A few libraries around the world hold an anonymous English translation published

I

two years later, but this new translation by the writer Michelle Bailat-Jones is a gift for which readers of the few works of Ramuz in English have waited decades.

*   *   *

A stranger has arrived in a fishing village, the beautiful Juliette. She is in mourning and hides for days in the innkeeper's house. When she emerges this Persephone brings in, in one day (a Thursday!), the entire Spring. The men look up, see her coming in her full beauty. An old fisherman is moved to doff his hat. Her effect on the men, then on the women, and gradually on every aspect of village routine, forms the book.

Is beauty a kind of natural disaster? Is it an anarchy, a drain on organized life? Is there a place for it and if so how much can it be allowed to usurp? Who gets to possess it? Why should it bring both delight and ruin?

The villagers do not ask these questions, but enact them. Ramuz is at once the chorus to their bursts of confused speech and a kind of ghost guide to everything that goes on, whether noticed by them or not. This wish to account for everything, from the serial positions a body gets into while climbing a wall to the movement of frogs, might drown narrative or take its place, and often in Ramuz it seems bent on doing so, but a real account is always going on, a tale.

Michelle Bailat-Jones has translated the novel with fidelity, blessed with the ear of someone who is a writer of fiction herself. As such she obeys the strictures of an original and rebellious stylist. Any translator of Ramuz's idiosyncratic French must deal with his experiments with tense and person. He will swerve from the completed past of realist fiction into a tense we could call the "dazzled present" for the distracted, distracting wonder it carries, which stalls the narrative and resets it over and over again in a slow syncopation. Likewise with seeming recklessness—but really with a constant deliberation we know of from his journals and essays—he will juggle the pronouns that establish point of view: "we," "I," "you." The scholar David Bevan, whose profound studies of Ramuz's work are a singular good fortune for the reader in English, calls this method "a global intuition which seeks to weld into a single person, author, reader, and character."

The home Ramuz prepares for this everyman, a tiny, seemingly eccentric locale, turns out to be a center from which the world rolls back on all sides, and thus a point where everything can be seen to converge. What takes place in a Swiss fishing village is what happens on earth, and even beyond—what happens to earth. His wish, he wrote to his Hungarian translator, was "to reconcile the region and the universe."

Thus his prose makes a slow outward sweep—looking for Cuba on a map the men find the geography of the world—and returns from "that huge illimitable space, those other endless waters," to examine the two fat men of the first scene, Rouge and Milliquet. We see their mustaches, the varicose veins and big shoes of one, the other's sweater that buttons on the shoulder. With his near-worship of detail, Ramuz—whose lack of interest in the interior man can seem cold—suspends us in the painful enterprise of these clumsy figures.

His is the imagination that closes in, fingers in a kind of enchantment the cloth of shawls, the mud on boots, the knots in rope, the dirt on an arm. Paradoxically it is an imagination eager to shake off the spell of the distinct—detail, dialogue, and even action—to revolve in the indistinct and vast, the still aspect of land and water seen from a distance, the seasons, and time itself. Nature in a Ramuz novel is not the environmentalists' refuge and project, but an unappeasable force, a slow cosmic rampage, mirrored in human rampages. The humans, like Juliette in her disruptive beauty, are pieces of this Nature and have victims of their own whether they mean to or not.

Are we ready for Ramuz, in our century? We are fast and he is slow. We stock fiction with the many-layered self, while for him character has little interest. "The more complex [a character] becomes," he says, "the less contact there is with the deep substance, one no longer gets past the bark." We are skeptics; to him "The need to believe is not the same as the need to understand." We are in transit, while he plants a man in one spot like a tree.

Yet if Ramuz stood above us on one of his hills he would be likely to see the same small figures—with their shameless violence, their longing for beauty—that he saw in the year of this novel, when the world was staggering back from World War I. We can only hope Michelle Bailat-Jones will go on bringing this vital oeuvre into English.

Valerie Trueblood
April 2013

Translator's Note

An English translation of Charles Ferdinand Ramuz's 1927 novel *La Beauté sur la Terre* was published in 1929 by G.P. Putnam's Sons. The translation is not signed and is quite typical of the time period in that it attempts to smooth away any elements of the text that might have been difficult for its English-language readers. It is not only a translation, but an edited version of Ramuz's original. Indeed, entire paragraphs are sometimes removed with the insertion of a few transitional words and often Ramuz's unique syntax was ignored or radically re-ordered. But the greatest "infidelity" to the original novel is how this 1929 translation subtly altered the ending of *La Beauté sur la Terre*. Putnam's English edition shortens the last page of the novel, removing some of the narrator's stage directions and pulling away from the final scene more quickly than Ramuz's original. It is still quite moving—the first English readers of this book were certainly not denied an understanding of the pathos of that last moment—but it does deny the reader a final Ramuzian hat trick, that of the narrator shifting away from his characters and stepping backward to become one of them himself.

That narrator is without a doubt the hardest element of *La Beauté sur la Terre* to pin down in translation. Not a fixed entity within the text or even outside of it, this strange yet compelling voice shifts and moves, transforming itself continuously as the story develops—moving outward, moving inward, inviting the reader inside of scenes and, even, at times, settling ambiguously in a narrative location that hovers between a single character and an entire village chorus.

The origin of this shifting narrative perspective is the particular way in which Charles Ferdinand Ramuz mixes the French pronouns *vous* and *nous* (*you* and *we*), how he allows the rare interjection of the first person *je*, as well as his peculiar use of the French indefinite pronoun *on*—a pronoun that does not quite exist in English. Here, as in much of Ramuz's work, what can normally be translated as *one* or *you* or *everyone*, depending on the context, is endowed with subtle but unexpected possibilities. Ramuz does one quite extraordinary thing with his *on*: he settles it from time to time onto individual characters in a technique that blurs the distinctions between their private thoughts and general human reactions or tendencies. In doing this, he creates a sliding scale of *he* or *she* and *you* and *we*, moving the reader into and outside the village and into different characters.

Ramuz initiates the reader to this narrative shifting quite slowly. The first chapter unfolds in a familiar-feeling omniscient, with only a hint of a villager-voiced *we* (taken from the *on*). But by the opening of the second chapter, the narrator embraces this *we* directly, avoiding the French *on* and choosing *nous*. At the end of this chapter, about ten pages into the entire story, Ramuz uses his *on* for the first time with respect to a single character: Milliquet—who is looking to see if there is a light on in Juliette's upstairs bedroom—walks out onto the terrace. The French is clear here, a third-person:

> *La nuit venue, Milliquet est allé voir sur la terrasse s'il n'y avait pas de la lumière dans sa chambre; il a vu qu'il n'y en avait point.*

When it was dark, Milliquet went to look from the terrace whether there was any light on in her room; he saw there was none.

But in the next sentence, he widens his lens:

> *Et on n'entendait aucun bruit, bien que le plancher fût un simple plancher de sapin sans tapis et que la chambre où couchaient les époux Milliquet se trouvât être juste au-dessous de la sienne.*

And no one heard the slightest sound, even though the floor in her room was simple pine planking without a carpet and the room where Mr. and Mrs. Milliquet slept was just below.

That *on* explodes off and away from Milliquet to embrace the narrator, the characters, and perhaps, the reader, as well. Not just "we" but suddenly, none of us are allowed to hear the slightest noise from that closed up window, behind which Juliette is sleeping. It is an unsettling movement, subtle but radical, and it is what defines Ramuz's style.

Also, the language of *La Beauté sur la Terre*, especially when Ramuz is describing a natural phenomenon like sunlight or water or the forests that surround this small lakeside village, relies on a keenly sensitive and unique system of metaphor and simile—in which the Alps shine like "upturned white ceramic cups" or the sunlight "places the night into the thickness of the branches" of a nearby forest. Or where the sky at night becomes wrinkled up wrapping paper and the boundaries of an open-air terrace lit at night with electric lamps become glass walls behind which the characters move.

Finally, Ramuz's prose loves to wind and jump about—it is not rambling, exactly, but ecstatic and detailed; his sentences are thickly layered with thought and image, and his punctuation style represents this kind of textured approach to storytelling. In this, as well as in his unconventional narrative perspective, I have chosen to remain faithful to the original French, even when it might be strange or confusing for an English-language reader. Ramuz's style is gently provocative, even for a Francophone and it would be a shame to deny an English reader the challenge of wandering about inside his exquisite universe.

Michelle Bailat-Jones
Puidoux, May 2013

I

"Just look," said the owner, "don't you see the stamp is from America? Santiago, on the island of Cuba. And this is an official letter, no mistaking that. What should I answer?"

"Well," Rouge said. "If I were you, I'd let her come."

"You think so?"

The two men were talking near the glass door which opened out onto the terrace and which was wide open, even if this was only March, because it was bright and sunny that day. They were the only two in the café. And Milliquet re-opened the letter, which was machine-typed and on letterhead, something which impressed him.

"No doubt... *Georges-Henri Milliquet, 54 years old, died 23 February 1927 at the Santiago de Cuba Hospital...* Georges-Henri, that's definitely my brother."

He continued reading aloud: *"To carry-out his last request... a sum of 363 dollars, subtracting travel costs, unless we receive notification of your refusal...* Oh! Rouge, what should I do?"

"How old is she?"

"Nineteen."

"That's a fine age."

"Yes," said Milliquet, "But God knows how she will have been raised and what habits she will have taken up in those hot countries, those Negro countries... there's also the problem of climate."

"Well, she'll arrive in summer."

"Sure, but..." he stammered, nodding his soft flabby

face; a face covered in folds which moved upward from his chin across his jowls like lines in a notebook. "It's just no one's heard from him (speaking of his brother) in at least 35 years; I've believed he was dead for a while now…"

"Well! Now you know he wasn't and you were wrong," Rouge said. "That happens. And it seems your brother didn't think the same of you since he's the one who gave your address to the consulate… And, you know, a brother is a brother… You can't just leave your niece to those Americans."

Milliquet shrugged his shoulders beneath a thick-cabled russet hunter's vest which he'd buttoned all wrong over a collarless shirt.

He said, "You see, only 363 dollars… and once we deduct the cost of the trip… what could a trip like that cost? And how long does it even take? You have any idea, do you?"

"Just look at the stamp."

"Three weeks. Okay, now count. The boat ticket, the train ticket, food, the hotel…"

"That's not the issue. If you abandon your niece, what will everyone think of you? And then this poor man, think a bit about him; picture yourself on your death bed… you've got no family, no friends, you're about to die, you're leaving a daughter behind; you're leaving a daughter behind and no money… Oh! Think about it, Milliquet, who else would you turn to at a time like that if not your family and your native land, even if you'd left it all behind a hundred years before? He said to himself, 'Luckily I have a brother… ' maybe he only had enough time to call the consul."

"But," said Milliquet, "he didn't even know my address." And he showed Rouge the envelope with its several corrections and messy ink-stains.

But Rouge answered, "What does that matter? I'm just telling you one thing, and that is that he died calmly because he believed he could count on you. Everything else doesn't..."

Milliquet sighed again; he brings his hand to his neck and rubs up and down a few times. "What is my wife going to say?"

Rouge emptied the rest of his three deciliter carafe into his glass; he doesn't answer. He had a fat red face, a brushed leather sailing cap with a visor and a nearly white mustache. He was wearing a blue knit wool turtleneck which buttoned on his shoulder. Short, fat and square, he was leaning forward on his stool and puffed from time to time on the pipe he held in the corner of his mouth.

He didn't answer, he only said, "Yes." He said it a second time.

Putting his pipe in the palm of his left hand, he took up his glass and emptied it; he clucked his tongue, he wiped his mouth with the back of his hand and said, "You haven't seen Décosterd by any chance?"

Milliquet shook his head.

"I've got to go see what he's doing." He gets up. And that's when he said, "The consul didn't tell you whether she was pretty?"

He tugged on his sweater which had rumpled around his heavy body and lifted one side to take out his wallet.

"As for your wife," he began again, "tell yourself you'll have a scene no matter what you do, but you're used to that... See you later."

He goes out through the terrace.

Milliquet was still holding the letter in his big chubby hand with its reddish hairs. The big bright sun was shining; the light reflected back off the lake. We could see the bare

3

branches of the plane trees stretched out horizontally from one tree to the next like the beams of a ceiling; they threw their shadows all the way onto the tables in the café where they broke in half on the table edges, throwing their remaining halves onto the floor boards. The light from the lake came in over the wall that bordered the terrace and hit the branches and the great green tree trunks from top to bottom. Milliquet took one step in his knitted slippers, then he took another: What to do? Oh Lord, what to do? He had a colorless little mustache and a sparse pale beard across his fat, drooping, brown-spotted cheeks.

He took another step forward with his right foot, and then with his left...

His wife would have definitely ended up suspecting something, so he was right to tell Rouge about the letter and the girl; if he needed it, Rouge could always give him a hand...

He moved his left foot, then his right. "And well, so be it, so be it. She should come... She..." He stopped himself for a second and then, speaking out loud again (now about his wife), "Well, her, she's a problem. Better deal with her right away."

He called, "Rosalie! Hey, Rosalie!"

Mrs. Milliquet appeared on the stairs.

And what happened next was that for the whole rest of the afternoon the neighbors were treated to a violent discussion.

It's this letter from America, and a niece that Milliquet had over there, and who's just dropped into his lap. In the village, though, we were all saying that he was right to say yes...

We were all saying it just like Rouge, "A brother is a brother..."

4

II

It took three weeks for Milliquet's answer to reach its destination, which brings us to the beginning of April; a bit later a dispatch from the consul told us that the young girl had gotten on the boat.

Milliquet had gone to borrow an atlas from the school teacher; he was flipping through it with Rouge.

They'd had to turn a lot of pages before they found America; America itself was divided into three parts.

An America in three parts; they'd hesitated before deciding on the right one.

It was at the bottom of a Gulf, on an island: and to the north was the United States colored red, to the west was Mexico in green, to the south was a purple-colored bend pointing straight back toward us like an arm:

"You see," Rouge was saying, "that's the Panama canal... Panama Bonds, don't you remember? No, you're too young... And you're right," he went back to another subject, "it's got to be half Negroes in those countries; you don't know who her mother was?"

"I don't know a thing, not a thing, not a thing..."

But at least it was easy to see she hadn't had to make a long journey to get on the boat.

"And then it heads toward us, but I don't know much about the route it takes..." Rouge was talking about the boat, tracing his finger toward the east. "Because it's filled with islands... if it goes between Cuba and Haiti, or between Santo Domingo and Puerto-Rico, or between

Puerto-Rico and the... wait..." He read the name on the map. "The Virgin Islands... to leave the Sea of Antilles; but then, no matter how it goes, you're in the Atlantic Ocean..."

He stopped himself once again. Having arrived at the edge of the map he had to flip back in the atlas to the page showing Africa, which looked like a huge turnip; the scale was not the same. Rouge blundered.

"Wait, we have to find the degree. The 20... there, look, just in front of the White Cape."

And there, finally, the ocean was wide open before us, and Rouge was trying to imagine it, because although we certainly have water, ours is small. A hundred kilometers at the most in one direction, ten or twelve in the other, a small bit of water, just a lake surrounded by mountains; and Rouge was trying to picture that huge illimitable space, those other endless waters, cut flat along the skyline like scissors cutting a blue cloth. In the picture he saw six white decks (he remembered images he had seen in magazines), smokestacks like towers.

"Oh," Rouge was saying, "it goes fast (because he was also a bit of a navigator). She should be nearly in the Canaries by now." He said, "These are turbine boats. They don't have paddlewheels like ours. On the ocean, the waves are much too large."

That boat was beneath ocean birds, while here we only have sparrows; it was under a scorching sun, here it was still cold, the fields were covered with a white frost in the morning and only the first violets were showing themselves beneath the hedges;—here yet were only a few steamboats on the lake and we had barely seen any sailboats either, because they don't like to come out too early.

Here, everything is small. We could see Rouge rowing in his boat and that's all we could see.

The water was gray, water like sand, or the color of soapy water; the sky was the same color as the water and made it hard to see the mountains.

In the café, we have opened the atlas again and the other men who were there drinking came over to join Milliquet and Rouge, leaning in to see between their shoulders:

"Today," Rouge was saying, "she must be arriving in the Strait of Gibraltar."

To locate the Strait of Gibraltar, they had to flip through the entire atlas again; they found Italy, then they found Spain; these pages had a reduced scale, so that Spain, for example, was bigger than Africa; but now Milliquet has taken Rouge to the side:

"You know I'm giving her the room upstairs, the south facing one. It's a good room…"

"You're right," said Rouge. "Better to do things conscientiously when you do them…"

Around this time a card arrived from Marseille; this time it wasn't the consul, it was the traveler herself who had written it.

"It appears," Milliquet said, "that she knows French… my brother will have taught her…"

It was raining. There were round puddles in front of the stables and between the cobblestones like the bottom of bowls filled with milky coffee. Milliquet took a boy with him who pushed a wheelbarrow. The village station here is small and the 2H40 train was an omnibus; the people who take it are always the same: villagers gone to town on business, traveling salesmen, cattle merchants in long black or purple shirts; there were only three or four and they all got down; Milliquet was standing near the front of the train. The travelers got down; already they were leaving the station; already the stationmaster, putting his whistle to his mouth, was ready to give the signal to go; that's when we saw the controller step hastily into one of the wagons and then reappear with a suitcase.

The train moved away quickly, while one by one the travelers took to the road.

Under his umbrella, Milliquet moved closer.

He moved closer in his big calfskin shoes with their brass eyelets which he dragged in the gravel; that day his varicose veins were giving him particular trouble; still moving forward, he turned around and gave a sign that the boy should follow him; and so, after this long waiting time (three weeks), across all these oceans and islands, and all the countries he'd glanced at (and also dreamed about, because finally Rouge and the atlas had piqued his imagination) – there was nothing before him on the train platform but a poor little gray thing.

A person without feet, or arms, all wrapped up in a hooded rain coat, and Milliquet couldn't even see her face. She barely raised her hand when he held out his own, saying:

"Well then! So how are you doing?"

Then he said:

"Did you have a nice trip? It was a bit long, no?"

She barely lifted her head; her suitcase was at her feet, an old leather suitcase all worn around the edges with a broken closure so that only the strap tightened around its bursting middle kept it from opening.

Now he walked next to his niece; he said nothing, she said nothing.

Behind them the boy held the wheelbarrow straight because the path leading to the village is steep. It was a wheelbarrow for grass. They passed under the railroad track; then, on your left, comes a large square house with an elm-tree bordered avenue that we all call the Chateau. It was raining, a delicate rain which seemed less like it was falling from the sky than floating in every which way in the air around you; and Milliquet was walking beneath his umbrella while the girl, the girl was walking beside him and hugging her coat around her;—next, on your right, comes some fields, some orchards, three or four large farms; after the Chateau on your left, there is a line of smaller houses, there's a pink house, there's a yellow house, there's a new house with a store; two or three people appeared on the steps of the store. But we must have thought there wasn't much to see, so much so that nothing was to be seen all the way to the road leading to the lake.

There, Milliquet stopped and said, "Here we are."

The front door opened, making way for Mrs. Milliquet's head beneath a black wool scarf.

Milliquet was carrying the suitcase. "Listen, Miss…" he said. Then he started again, dropping the title, "Listen, I'll take you directly to your room. You must be tired."

He went before her along the yellow-painted hallway; together, they went up two stories. They arrived in front of a rough pine door opposite an identical door.

Milliquet opened the door and said, "Here you are. This is your room."

He placed the suitcase in front of the bed on a carpet with the image of a black and white dog with its tongue hanging out.

"If you need anything, all you have to do is call."

Rouge came just a bit later, to be discreet.

"So?"

"So, she's here."

Rouge sat at his normal spot in the café; hesitantly, he spoke again, "And so, how is she?" He raised his head toward Milliquet but Milliquet shrugged his shoulders.

"How should I know?" And then just after, "What would you like to drink?"

He seemed annoyed, which surprised Rouge.

"How do you expect me to tell you," Milliquet started again. "She didn't open her mouth."

"Maybe it's a language problem."

"But she understands me very well."

"Three deciliters of the new," said Rouge.

Sometimes he took the old wine, sometimes the new; it depended on the weather, or his mood; sometimes he took three deciliters, sometimes a half.

The view on the water that day extended hardly farther than 300 meters until suddenly it was like a curtain falling from its rod in heavy folds.

Milliquet came back with the glass and the carafe, Rouge kept quiet.

Milliquet stared through the window at the cheerless curtains of fog which came across the lake one after the other, like a hand was bringing them and arranging them along a hanging rod;—eventually a question was asked behind his back (it took Rouge a long time to ask it).

"And otherwise?"

Milliquet looked at Rouge over his shoulder.

"I mean, how does she look like?"

"I couldn't say."

That was all.

At six o'clock, Milliquet had the serving girl bring her some coffee with milk; she didn't show herself the entire day.

When it was dark, Milliquet went to look from the terrace whether there was any light on in her room; he saw there was none. And no one heard the slightest sound, even though the planking in her room was simple pine without a carpet and the room where Mr. and Mrs. Milliquet slept was just below. Not the slightest creaking up there; they couldn't hear her walk or move; so when Milliquet closed up and went to join his wife, she said, "What is that girl doing? You're sure she didn't escape?"

III

Several days then passed, and the only thing that happened was that the next morning Milliquet went to ask her for her papers.

They were in order.

The consul had organized them himself in a large yellow envelope wrapped with a rubber band; she had handed the envelope to Milliquet without saying a word.

She was dressed. She had a black handkerchief around her head. She was seated on a small straw chair.

"This is so everything is in order, you understand. I'm going to go see the municipal secretary. If by chance there is anything missing, he would tell me…"

She didn't move at all; during this time, Milliquet stood in the middle of the room and busied himself with looking through the envelope, pulling on the rubber band with his fat red-haired fingers.

"Here's your birth certificate, that's good… Oh! You won't be twenty until next March. For the time being, I'll be your guardian, but I'll still have to get that settled…"

He continued rifling through the papers.

The birth certificate, passport, letters of recommendation, his own address, written in large, carefully-formed letters at the end of an itinerary, with the title: *place of destination* – nothing more, no mention of money; and he asked again, "Is this all?" the remains of his scruples preventing him from daring to be more precise: she nodded her head again, without saying a word.

She seemed to be cold, she was holding herself tightly in her shawl. It was clear she hadn't yet unpacked her suitcase and it gaped open at the base of the wall. And Milliquet looked at his niece again, but he must have thought it would be better not to insist for the moment; she had certainly not yet recovered from the weariness of her trip; he slipped the envelope into his pocket, "Okay, it's understood. I'll take it over then." Then, as he left, he contented himself with saying, "And then, when you'd like, you can come downstairs. You've got to meet your aunt. She's waiting for you."

The Milliquets took their meals in the kitchen; they'd set a place for her; at noon, they called up for her but she didn't come.

"Are you going to keep taking your young lady her food in her room?" asked Mrs. Milliquet. "A lodger! That's what she is. Well, if you've got the money…"

And the serving girl, a fat, disheveled girl with dirty arms, shoved the cutlery around on the platter, "Two floors three times a day! I should have been warned…"

"Besides," she added to Mrs. Milliquet, "for what she eats! That's not only wasted time, that's what I call 'tortured' food."

However, a great change was preparing itself in the air and on the other side of the water on the mountain. Rouge, who came every day (it was an old habit) stopped himself at the edge of the door, and, raising his head, said, "This time I think we're set for some real fine weather." It was Thursday. Leaving, he raised his head and noticed that the phenomenon up on the mountain was more than a change in weather, it was the entire season changing. Rouge added nothing to his remark; it wasn't that he wasn't intrigued, and he wasn't the only one, as no one in the neighborhood or the café regulars, nor any of the people who had come out of curiosity in those first few days, had yet seen the young lady, but when anyone said to Milliquet, "So, about this niece?" he answered, "She's resting."

So Rouge, too, had to be content with this answer. People were saying in the village, "The young lady is certainly a quiet one." At the same time, a ladder of sunshine had descended from a hole in the sky, like a boat throwing a rope to someone cast overboard. To get home, Rouge had to follow the shoreline which hugged the fields, then some pine tree woods. There, a new voice came to him from deep in the forest. When the cuckoo sings, the girls say to each other, "Do you have any money in your wallet?" and when the answer is yes, it's a good sign, because it means you'll have money for the entire year. Up in the mountains, the south wind was fighting with the north wind. Down on the lake, the cuckoo was singing. Then the clouds moved all together and began to tumble about, rolling on top of each other where the sky inclined toward the south. By Saturday the sky was completely clear; meaning that everywhere in the village at the same time everyone was making themselves nice for Sunday. It's more than a change in weather, it's even more than a change of season: everything makes itself beautiful up there like never before, up above the Dents d'Oche, on its points and peaks. On the Cornettes, on the Billiat, on the Voirons, on the Môle, the Salonné; in the gorges, on the plateaus, all around the rock walls and the pasture land. Everyone has picked up their great birch broom, the great hard birch broom we use in the stables; next, we go with the straw brooms and the flat brush. And everywhere above you, because of the snow, the mountains were shining like upturned white ceramic cups, like the tops of plates. Nothing but a few little clouds, pushed quickly toward the south above the mountain range, just a few tiny sailcloths filled with wind and which vanish at an angle, while below, on the water, there was also this little sail, and it looked like one of those clouds, one of those tiny little clouds left behind and fallen down; it was Rouge who was taking advantage of the weather to go out in the boat with Décosterd...

Saturday afternoon, Milliquet was busy taking out the benches and tables from the storage shed where he kept them for the winter. The serving girl had helped him, but not without making him understand that this wasn't her job. They had gone together behind the house to get the heavy, green-painted wooden tables which they carried each at an end. From time to time, Milliquet raised his eyes toward two small windows on the second floor, but they stayed closed. While he rested a moment, the serving girl next to him, in her gray flannel caraco which was badly buttoned across her big chest, was breathing heavily with her hand splayed flat on her kidneys. The terrace was extremely important to Milliquet, especially on Sundays when the weather was fine, because of people strolling along; and these days a lot of shopkeepers had their own car or a little truck which could be converted into a Sunday car. Since already his establishment wasn't doing as well as it should have (a manner of speaking), he made sure never to miss this extra profit. And so he re-attached himself to one of those six long tables, much too long and heavy, he noticed now, because they were kitchen tables, but he'd gotten them second hand for cheap, and had repainted them himself to make garden tables.

It was underneath the plane trees which stood behind the wall of the river walk, over which we could see the water, and we could also see a part of the mountain between the wall and the heavy branches which flattened out above you.

Later in the season, when they were adorned with leaves, they became like a ceiling that not even the sun, nor a glance, could penetrate. But for now, they were still naked and looked like thick, age-worn beams that the heat had warped and twisted in every direction, with swollen spots and black holes and cracks. With their forked ends and criss-crossings, they made a kind of pattern above your head framing diamond-shaped pieces of sky; the pattern was black, the diamonds blue. The sun came; the trees weren't yet completely dry on their lower half.

It was Sunday, it was Milliquet's terrace, a terrace with a view on the lake to the front, to the east toward a street, and to the west toward a smaller street, on the other side of which some people were playing ninepins. Here, we are sheltered from the north wind, and as the sun turned itself toward us, it became warmer in the still air, while the wind fell further out on the lake making a thousand little ripples which escaped out toward the larger expanse of water.

After eleven o'clock, the game of ninepins grew noisy; we could see above the wall that the players had taken off their jackets. They'd removed their iron gray Sunday jackets; they were wearing clean white shirts they'd put on that morning. The ninepins were tumbling down like a burst of laughter. In the café were those who'd come to drink their aperitif and there were more people than usual because the weather was so fine (and maybe also for another reason). Those who were playing ninepins were drinking where they played; we were drinking with the game of ninepins and we were drinking in the café. The serving girl was coming and going; Milliquet was coming and going; Mrs. Milliquet herself finally put in an appearance;—up above, no one had yet moved, while the mist cleared beneath the branches of the plane trees, while the terrace slowly lost its humidity.

The noon bells ring.

Now it is Rouge who begins to speak. Rouge was saying, "As for me, I came at two o'clock with Décosterd. On Sundays, I buy him a drink."

"The terrace," Rouge was saying, "was already half full with people we didn't know; these weren't people from around here. The café was also pretty full and there we were among friends; but what I mean is, or what I'm about to say is that Milliquet had a lot to do (it's good for him, this doesn't happen every day). He was serving in the café, the serving girl was serving on the terrace; as for Milliquet's wife, she was scolding in the kitchen. We could tell right away there was once again some trouble in the house, even if, at least for him, the job suited him well, and even too well. But for many people too much or not enough is all the same; they complain for the famine and they complain for the feast, because happiness comes from within and a person either carries their own happiness or they don't. This was when the serving girl, who was running, dropped a glass. Right when Mrs. Milliquet arrived.

She started to yell, "This is not a life…"

Milliquet said, "What do you want me to do about it?"

The rest of us in the café were having fun. There were about ten of us, but she didn't really care, because, when she's got an idea in her head, she won't let go for anything. "What do I want? Ah, well, let's talk about it… when someone is worn out already first thing in the morning and going to be just as exhausted in the afternoon, and all evening and up to midnight or one o'clock at fifty-three years old, and there's this *missy* upstairs…"

All the while people were calling to Milliquet and he was saying to his wife, "Be quiet! Be quiet, won't you… Yes, I'm coming…"

"A *missy* who had to have her dinner again in her room, a day like today, say it's not true, come on, tell these men it's not true if you dare… yes, sirs, we brought up dinner to this tiresome girl, that's what I'm saying…"And she kept going because once she's gotten started, it was never a short complaint; so Milliquet made up his mind. He served one more customer, then I watched him go out by the hallway door…"

She'd gone back to stretch out on her bed. She got up and went to sit in a chair, she didn't know why she was sitting; she went back to lie on the bed, she didn't know why she was lying down. In her mind was a great jumble of images coming and going in every direction; then one of the images grew and placed itself before the others; it was a boat deck. And then an oiled cloth with a plate and a glass, or a fat lady with a yellow and white armband, her gray jacket cinched at the waist and buttoned over a guimpe with a high collar. One of the woman's whalebone corset stays entered into a fold of skin beneath her chin each time she opened her mouth… The wall in front of her has gray paper with little white roses. The wall comes to her through the other image which grew smaller and became transparent like when the weft of a cloth becomes worn. Having gotten up, she goes to the wall to touch it. Then she moves again to the chair, again she balances herself, the chair rising slowly beneath her to then descend again even further, and all the while she feels a coldness around her heart. It seemed to her that night had come. She heard the horns screaming in the fog. Someone knocks and the door opens. She sees, without raising the head that she's hidden in her hands, she sees between her fingers that they've brought her a meal on a tray; then she must have cried again for a long time; she must have slept, must have slept for a long time; it's impossible to tell when a person has started to sleep or finished sleeping. The nights and the days have all mixed together, like lacing the fingers of one hand with the other hand. She is here, but, at the same time, she sees the hospital, a pot of tea, the iron bed, the white sheets, the night light, the temperature sheet fixed to the wall with thumbtacks; —she hears the rain fall on the roof, she hears the sparrows tapping their beaks against the gutters with little dry pecks or even the squeak of the tinplate under their claws;—and now? Oh, they've buried him! Then they take her into some offices. She goes to a photographer, they glued her photograph onto a page of a notebook; they affixed a wet seal to half of her photograph and half of the written page. She cries a great deal again. She's cold. She stretches out on her bed; she rolls herself up in her blankets. She finds herself in a train wagon very close to the engine; the engine whistles, whistles again, the brakes grind against the wheels; a jolt, the train stops abruptly...

"Juliette!"

She recognizes the name her father gave her; then someone has tried to open the door, but the door is locked.

"Juliette, will you answer?"

The person tries again, "You've locked yourself in now. What is this kind of behavior? This can't go on much longer... You're going to come down. We need you..."

She had seated herself on the bed; she said, "I'm coming." She finds herself seated on the bed, surprised. The person went back down the stairs. She is surprised because it suddenly seems to be daylight. The wall in front of her has changed color. She wonders first if she isn't still dreaming, but she sees that it stays, the wall remains before her;—it moves and at the same time the ceiling moves. A number of pretty little moons are up there, having all the same movement, like they were sewn one to another: they make her think of a lace pattern, while a square of sunlight comes across like a carpet on the wooden floor. And these things are all real. There is also a warmth which comes to her; she throws off the blanket she'd had wrapped around her. She is like a person just waking up, and this time it's for good. The burst of laughter of the ninepins outside makes her turn her head toward the two small windows which face the front of the room beneath the roof; here, she is again surprised. She can see nothing at first, because there are two lights: the light from above and the light from below, from the sky and from the water. We were playing ninepins, we were tapping with a glass or a carafe on the tables, there were loud conversations going on all around, we were calling the owner;—in the windows was all that water burning in rows of sparkles, and burning white like a fire of wood chips. Below is the water, but there are three things. The water is below, then she looks a little higher and sees the land (if it is truly land on that other bank, when it looks more like sculpted air, air which has been squeezed between your hands). It was like air surrounded by air, blue surrounded by blue, until higher up, but then she didn't understand at all anymore: up there the beautiful laundry-like fields of snow were hanging on a rope of sky…

"And that was when," Rouge was saying, "Rossi's workman began to play. It has to be said that he's an artist, not two like him in the area. And the instrument! An instrument with twelve bass notes in exotic wood, sculpted with flowers so real you'd like to pick them… An instrument which costs five hundred francs at least, and you've got to hear the details of the high notes; a goldfinch couldn't do better. And an instrument like that can be heard a good kilometer away. The proof is that she heard it up in her room, and she was even lying down and she heard it from her bed (he was making things up now). It's the music that got her to get up, the music that brought her downstairs. Milliquet alone couldn't have done it. If he says different, he's bragging. Without the music, I swear, she would never have moved; in fact, she's the one who told me. And then, remember, when she arrived... we could all see why she was coming and for whom. A girl like that and music just go together. No one had seen her yet, and until that day she was like a dead person; but there you go, girls are just like that: a little dance tune will revive them. It's because of the countries where they come from, warm countries. You just have to remember the way she came in..."

Mrs. Milliquet was coming out of the kitchen and just closing the door. Her hand stayed motionless on the doorknob; the noise of voices in the café came to a halt like someone had cut the sound with a pair of scissors.

There wasn't a single noise behind the corridor wall where it was like a first wave of silence, in front of which the noise from the terrace continued to be heard, until it was silenced in its turn.

For a moment there was nothing but the rolling of a ball on the well-oiled plank, like when a storm begins; then the burst of the ninepins; then, "Four... ?" Into the deep silence, a voice said, "Four..."

"No, five... oh, yes, five... I didn't have..."

Then also over at the game everything was interrupted.

This was as she walked up to just beneath the plane trees.

The silence still lingered in the café.

She looked around her, at first she turned her back to the windows, then she turns toward the windows and the sunshine,—this is the moment when Chauvy stood up.

Like usual he was wearing his old bowler hat, his piss-colored jacket with its hodgepodge of buttons all sewn with string, his little cane, and his broken shoes; he walks forward and stands himself before her.

He puts his hand to his hat.

He doffs his hat, while his huge dirty beard dips forward toward the floor and was replaced by his bald pate shining between two tufts of hair.

IV

The general feeling was that Milliquet had made a good deal. If his hope of inheriting a nice sum of dollars had definitively evaporated, he was at least compensated by a substantial influx of francs which was not only imagined, nor imaginary, but already making a weight in his pocket, making a lovely light noise in the dip of his hand. In less than a week, his clientele had doubled—this was clear to him. And this was clear to everyone because we were all coming, and we kept coming, and those who could come in came in; but there were those that, because of their gender or their age, or a lack of money, were forced to stay outside; and these people watched through the bubble-filled windows, between the fake lace curtains, trying to see if she was there.

All they could see was that the café was full of smoke so thick you could cut it with a knife, as we say, because of course everyone was smoking cigars, cigarettes, clay pipes or wooden pipes, smoking beneath the low ceiling, in the little space there was between the ceiling and the floor, where it was all dark;—but maybe it was also because she was no longer shining.

This was happening at that time when the trees were all working together above the paths, working to hide the sky with their leaves; we could see the sparrows resting on the shutters, a long strip of straw in their beaks.

This was happening at that time when in just a few days the grass grows all the way up to your knees, as high as it will grow; the automobiles began to pass again in great numbers along the road, several coming from abroad (where she came from herself), with license plates written in black capital letters on white backgrounds, A., or GB. or Z. Up behind the village, there was the international road which was no longer a white road like the valiant car roads of yesterday, but all black with tar over the fine-grained sand which the tires smash to bits. Pieces of the world came to us up there at high speed, going with their white lights to rustle the trees in the orchard over the top of the hedge like taking a stick to knock down the fruits. And it shined there now with reflections on the hoods, on the windshield, on the nickel, the steel, the glass; the girl, the girl had nothing but a little black dress, with a black lace handkerchief tied around her hair (which we thought must have been the fashion in the country where she came from).

It didn't matter, people continued to come. The first words which had flown through the air had painted her in another way and with beautiful colors; that description still served. They continued to have an effect far away and to call people, so much so that all that time, when Milliquet did his accounting (and, quite simply, after closing his restaurant he went to the cash drawer to establish how many bills and coins had entered it throughout the day), he had cause to celebrate, or he would have had cause to celebrate, without his bad moods and his worries. Only now his wife had refused to be nice to Juliette, she had said to the serving girl, "It's worse than I thought." And Juliette was eating in the kitchen now, but Mrs. Milliquet wasn't giving the impression that she noticed she was there, which was the attitude she had adopted; pretending not to see Juliette come in, pretending not to hear when Juliette wished her good day, and sometimes raising her voice to complain or make an insulting comment, but she addressed herself only to her husband, who said nothing because this is easier.

The girl was not speaking anymore either. She lowered her head beneath her lace handkerchief. To see her face we had to lean down to the table; we tried to see her from beneath by stretching our necks out, which made everyone laugh (above the brown painted tables, because they were old furnishings), but sometimes we didn't laugh; above the filled or half-filled glasses in the smoke. We were laughing. All of a sudden we stopped laughing. We grew timid. This was when she raised her head. If we had started to say something, we grew quiet.

And now they no longer dared look her in the face, because it felt then like a long knitting needle entering your heart.

She served in the café, the serving girl on the terrace; Milliquet probably preferred keeping her near him, under his immediate supervision. When someone called from outside, he sent the serving girl.

One evening, a whole group of young people came. The days were beginning to get long, and after supper they still had time to go play a game of ninepins, or at least this was the pretext they gave themselves that evening. At first they came onto the terrace, then, having looked around them, and not having seen what they were looking for, they continued their way up to where the balls seemed to be waiting for them in the planks where they rolled back down and where they sat, the big one and the little one, with a round hole for your thumb, and a larger opening for your fingers.

Big Alexis looks over the wall on the terrace side. "What should we order?" He hits the table with his fist.

Amidst the ninepins game, that night, big Alexis, the dragon, a handsome boy of more than six feet tall, with a little blond mustache, a low forehead, and curly hair;—he hits the table then with all his strength.

The serving girl arrives.

No one had started to play yet; we heard the serving girl saying, "What would you like?"

Alexis answered, "Nothing."

He picks up the biggest of the balls and says to Gavillet, "It's your throw."

Gavillet plays his turn.

And the serving girl who's been waiting finally leaves, without understanding what was happening, or not yet understanding; so Alexis grabbed a stick which was lying about and hit the table again to make sure he was heard.

He watched who was going to come; the fat serving girl is the one who comes back.

He stayed facing her until she came up, then said, "What are you doing here, you?"

"Rude boy!"

She left; we heard her voice on the terrace, and then Milliquet himself came out.

"Oh, it's you!" said Alexis. "It's just you... well, that isn't what we want." And to the others he said, "Let's get out of here...we'll come another time."

They passed across the terrace again; with them was little Maurice Busset, our mayor's son, who was not yet 18 years old, and had a soft and reserved character; we all pretty much understood that he was already engaged.

Rouge was now coming twice a day. That day he had come for the first time around 2:00; he came back later in the evening, when the first quarter of the moon had begun to show itself above the peaks of the Oche or the peak of the Oche (because really, for us, there is only one).

The clouds had been hanging a long time in the sky like a layer of dirty ice; suddenly they broke up in all directions.

Seen through the holes, the sky looked like little rivers up there, like an irrigated field. Rouge, pushing through the door to the café, was surprised to see that it was empty. He waits a moment: no one comes. He waits, then he hears the noise of a discussion coming from the kitchen, and, through the walls, he recognizes Milliquet's voice, then he recognizes the voice of the serving girl. Still no one was coming; he had to call. He had to open the door which led to the corridor, and he had to yell out, "Hey, is anybody here?" Then the sound of the voices stopped suddenly, and Milliquet appeared; but, seeing Rouge, he dropped his head into his two hands.

"What's happened?"

Milliquet came beneath the lamp, his face much grayer and more wrinkled than usual, his head sideways, his mouth half open. "What's happened?" Then, he said, "You know, this is all your fault... as if there weren't already enough women here, but no, you had to go and bring me a third one... just look." He gestured at the empty café. "No one could stand it..."

"My dear Milliquet, you never change. You don't see your own luck."

"My luck? Look..." He took a piece of paper out of the pocket of his hunting vest.

"Look," said Milliquet, holding out to Rouge a piece of notebook paper with a column for adding numbers.

Help Wanted

This was the title; beneath it were several lines written in thick letters filled with scratch-outs.

In a small respectable lakeside establishment, young girl with good references to work in the café. Apply to the following number...

"Exactly," said Milliquet, "you see what it's come to. I didn't even dare put my name."

He was standing beside the table, (tall, heavy, his trousers sagging, his sparse beard, and a yellowing mustache);—then suddenly, behind the ninepins game, beneath the sky which was getting clearer and clearer, although here we are beneath the lamps, suddenly the accordion began to play.

This was while Rouge, having finished reading, handed the paper back to Milliquet, and said, "What does that bother you? Look...you're used to women." This was beneath the electric lights, and Rouge kept talking, "You'll never change your wife, what do you want? Let her yell..."

Beneath the stained light bulbs, the three or four light bulbs stained with fly droppings and the cloth lampshade, which was also covered in the same little black dots.

"Sit down," said Rouge, "I'll explain it to you... but the girl, where is she?"

Milliquet shrugged his shoulders, "By Jove, she's in her room. She's locked herself in her room again. My wife has locked herself in *hers*... and the serving girl gave me her eight days notice."

He sat down, he put his elbows on the table and his head in his hands. "If this continues, I'll go crazy."

"No," said Rouge, "You've got something better to do. You're lucky, I told you, and don't make me take it back. You just need to know how to manage it..."

Up above, she had raised her head. She was only just half undressed. She was sitting on her bed. The moon was invisible. In front of her were two windows, so close together they touched; but the moon stayed hidden. On the other side of the windows, against the breaking up of the clouds, the moon was making a kind of very soft dusty light, like a light shining through a thin cloth. And the little notes of the accordion were coming. They passed through the window panes, shaking them just a little, like a bird on the wing. The girl had put her bare feet in her hands, stretched her neck out and was leaning forward. The notes kept coming, kept coming and coming; she jumps up onto the floor.

"You don't know how to make the best of it. Just let your wife keep yelling..."

She made it all the way to the door. She listens, her ear stuck against the thin panel of pine. No other sound could be heard in the house but a dull murmuring coming from the entryway, like a fly stuck behind a window...

"It isn't your wife who counts; look Milliquet, you know..."

She goes to her heavy leather suitcase; she pulls out a pair of espadrilles, a floral shawl which she wraps about herself; she slides out onto the landing. No one on the landing, and no one on the stairs. No one had yet lit the electric lamps or maybe Mrs. Milliquet had turned them off when she went to bed. The girl could easily get to the door which leads out to the little street, where the little notes were coming from. And, in fact, here they are again, stronger now, louder now in the fresh night, and more numerous: a dance tune which moves around her, and even enters into the corridor at the moment that she opens the door to the house...

"Leave her free," Rouge was saying in the cafe. "What do you want to make her work for? She isn't made for that. Leave her free, and then there's no risk of extinguishing her..."

The accordion came and played a moment around the two men, and it turned a moment beneath the cloth lampshade.

"It's like butterfly wings: if you touch them, they turn gray... let her run about... when you don't know what to do anymore, just send her to me."

But the door to the house had closed again. The girl was now on the other side of the door, in other words, on the good side. She had all the music for herself. All she needed to do was swim up it, like she would have swum up a stream. Just past the ninepins game was a kind of passage which opened up between two walls behind some sheds. She entered into the passage. She raises her head, turning it right and left. It was on the right. The wall was taller than her, but now we begin to see who she is. A wagon with a ladder had been pushed against the wall; she grabbed ahold of it with two hands, having wrapped her shawl around her belt, and then began to climb up the ladder, in the moonlight, because the moon had just come out from behind the clouds, and so the moon was on her hair, on her shoulders, then on her skirt and around her legs. We saw how flexible she was. She held herself crouched for an instant at the top of the wall, leaning forward on her hands which she held flat before her; she was on the edge of a paved terrace used for hanging out the washing, which we could see by the iron lines fixed between two supports. We saw that she knew what she was doing. We saw that she knew how to take care of herself. She did not stand up, did not straighten herself; that would have made it too easy to see her. That first quarter of the moon shone like a well-washed ice cube over the Café Milliquet, shining even farther out on the water like a kind of long road casting back its reflection; she crawled like a cat. She was so quiet that she seemed to add to the silence with her crawling. She made it to the other side of the terrace. All she had to do was stretch along it with her body, with only her eyes peeking out.

And so it was on the other side of a courtyard, in a long low house whose first floor only was made of stone. Something like a barn with a stable below and next to this stable were two rooms, one with the window lit up and no curtains. We could see him very well. Pushed back against the whitewashed walls, the room had a little iron bed with a brown blanket with a striped border; the boy was seated between the window and the bed, on a chair without a back, because he could not have been seated on a chair with a back. The hump on his back pushed his head down toward his knees; it was very difficult for him to raise it. Oh, he's so small! Oh, he's so pale! He's so small and he has this enormous instrument, an instrument which becomes even bigger than him when he pulls the red leather of the bellows completely open, then he bends it down into a half-circle, pushing on the pressed air from both sides; this is why he leans over with his entire body, and pulls his shoulders inward pressing on his open arms; how his fingers run quickly over the beautiful shiny keys! She moves her head forward a little. And then without seeing her, he turns toward her. With his foot he shifts the stool beneath him and begins a new song now that the other has finished: this time, it's the right song, this time, it's the most beautiful song;—it begins with a long call, a long cry held by the bass notes, then, there is a short silence; and then a thousand little notes tumble and crash against each other.

She had knocked at the window, he hadn't stopped. She knocks three times on the window, he simply raises his head, he doesn't seem surprised.

Nothing stops, nothing even changes, not the smallest instant, or slowing of the lovely movement of the bellows, his fingers which fly from top to bottom and from bottom to top, climbing and ascending the scale;—she knocks, he makes a sign that she can come in, then he leans again as hard as he can on the pressed air for a great chord; while the girl enters into a first room, where she is taken at the throat by the bitter odor of leather, making her cough, but she could see a small thread of light flickering below the second door.

At first she stood with both shoulders against the wall. She seemed very big compared to him.

She seemed to be trying to hold herself back, having thrown herself backward so far, her two shoulders against the wall, one hand on top of the other hand; then, suddenly, in the shadow, beneath her brown face, the great flash of her teeth appeared.

He must have understood; he made her a sign.

And the girl unwrapped her shawl from over her beautiful arms; she unwrapped it from around her curved neck.

V

Here, along the lake edge, it's a fairly flat region (and flat regions are rare in our country).

Here, the mountain holds itself back farther from the edge of the water, which elsewhere it borders tightly. It's a fairly flat piece of shoreline, although still somewhat bumpy, and it stretches wide for a kilometer or two.

Between the railway line and the water, there is a strange mix of still-wild fields and some crops (something rare around here). It's half farmer, half wine grower, with just a few large plots, as we say, not many big farms and not even many big houses, because here they are generally smaller than in the rest of the country. And a little farther out, toward the east, the land becomes impossible to cultivate; there, we find ourselves first on a fine sand beach with a forest of pine trees that comes down to die along the water; beside the shiny water, the foliage looks like a piece of the night. We were walking along this forest; the cuckoo was singing up above in the ravine. We can see the red tree trunks holding themselves up next to you into the sky like a kind of black ceiling; it's as if when the daylight comes upon the shiny water, the night is placed into the thickness of the branches. Someone has put it there at dawn to then take it out again near evening. Then, just farther than the wood, the sand stops and becomes little stones, but this time the shoreline widens rapidly, because of a peninsula that it pushes out towards the wide lake. We passed in front of Rouge's house which was less of a house and more of a kind of single-story shed, half wood and half brick, long ago painted yellow, and preceeded by a smaller shed for the net poles; to go further, one has to walk through two walls of reeds which are higher than your shoulders. Which brings us to the Bourdonnette. And there, the water is in front of you, where before it had been always beside you; but it was only a weak width of water, and dominated on the other shore by a steep cliff. It was dead water, water without any current. The bit of earth that stuck out on the sunset side sheltered it from any waves coming from Geneva, while the cliff protected it from any gusts of the east wind, the Vaudaire. There sat Rouge's boats (in the small path he cut back each year with a pruning knife); two rowboats, the smaller one painted green.

Both boats were there, tied with their ropes, above the shallow, pure water where a small fish resting on its belly moved itself around with regular movements back and forth like a ferry; the water would quickly grow murky because of the mud when you walked in, something you had to do if you wanted to go any further. You had to take off your shoes if you wanted to go as far as the cliff and its summit which is a lovely lookout spot; and, amidst the hot gravel there were all kinds of spiny tufts of grass, until you reached the green moss and its wet thickness beneath the great pine trees up above. Up there are the Great Woods, as we call them, even if they aren't very big, only thick and on the Bourdonnette side they are extremely steep and rough, while on the lake side they lean out over the emptiness; — there are plenty of couples and walkers, on Sundays.

From up there you could see Rouge's house very well.

We were just above it, when we turned towards the west. His two colored roof, half-shingled, half-tarpaper, looked like it was just set onto the sand. It seemed like just by jumping we could land into one of the two boats, like they were put there to catch you. We could see Rouge really well, as he went back and forth across the shoreline. That morning in particular, we could see him perfectly; this was just after he and Décosterd had come back from fishing.

Rouge was in front of his house with Décosterd; he was short and fat, Décosterd taller, skinnier.

We could easily see that Rouge had his arms crossed over his navy blue wool sweater; we could even see the light blue smoke from his pipe rising up around his face and about his dark blue shoulders.

It was all happening up there on the cliff, in this early June, when the Great Woods behind you were still full of the songs of birds in their caves, above the light green moss that smelled so strong. The moss smelled damp and fresh until you got among the dry rocks, while elsewhere the water shone dry and with glints of metal beneath new tin plating. The two men were only two black spots, they continued to be nothing but two black spots, seen from above and all flat; they were made into two oval spots on the gray rocks (seen closer these rocks were pink, light blue, purple, white). And again Rouge, his arms crossed, nodded his head beneath his cap, while the bird song came like an explosion, like someone firing a mortar, making the windows tremble in their putty. This great noise came from the land while there was nothing on the water but silence, only a small wave with a shiny hem, then with a rounded top, rolls upon the shoreline from time to time and then pulls itself back with a show of its claws.

Rouge, with his arms crossed, was studying his home.

He was studying the wooden shed which was attached to the stone part of the house, with one room and a kitchen, and then he started to speak, "Hey, Décosterd, what do you think of that?"

And then answering the question himself, "I don't think it's at all good…"

He points to the planks of the shed, once carefully jointed and stained, but which had been worn by the sun, and the rain, and the succession of the seasons, from cold and from warm, from both good and bad weather, and which had ended up shifting and were falling apart. He points to a kind of skin sickness on them that makes their color flake away, the door opening crookedly on its bent hinges; he shows the crumbling brick wall;—and what was strange about it was that the whole time he seemed content; he was saying "It's disgusting..." all while this contentment is shining in his eyes.

"Yes, Décosterd, that's how it is, we're getting old..."

The contentment is shimmering in his eyes while he puffs away on his pipe.

"It was all falling down... we paid it no mind, another way of saying that we were also falling down..."

He was saying these things in the past tense (why the past?); he started talking again, "And what about you, Décosterd? What do you think about it?"

Décosterd answers by moving his head. He hardly ever spoke. He motions that he was of this same opinion, with his good eye and his bad eye, beneath his gray cloth hat; but he's surprised all the same to see the boss in front of this old building and this falling down shed; he's even more surprised when Rouge turns to him and says, "Okay, Décosterd, go grab a meterstick."

Rouge takes a match to clean out his pipe and then he taps it in the cup of his hand, all while Décosterd has gone to get the meterstick.

Rouge slips his pipe into his pocket.

He takes the meterstick, he unfolds it.

"We'll see about this. Oh, it's a quick job, it is."

He walks up to the wall, saying, "It's thirty years old, you know, but we'll take some years off... 4 m 60, 4 m 60 by... by 3... and then," he says.

He stops, "Three and three and a half, that makes six, six and a half... that's for the repairs. Go get a pencil and some paper." He yells, "On the table... one of those catalogues... "

He goes and sits himself on the window sill and using the pencil he writes on the paper: "You see... the shed, my room, the kitchen... that's all for repair... but, right now, who would stop us from building a second room just next to the kitchen? We're certainly not short on space! Another room could certainly be useful if we need it... "

And he drew the map with his pencil on the paper.

"Three meters and a half by three, that would just about do it. All we have to do is drill a door in the wall of the kitchen, while we're at it. What do you think?"

"Of course."

"And you'd know what to do, wouldn't you?"

Because Décosterd had done a bit of everything, one profession at a time depending on the situation, field hand, digger, winemaker, mason.

"You'd know what to do, I'd help you."

"Oh, for sure," Décosterd was saying.

"And it'll be easy, of course, because we can get what we need right here, I'll just need to stop by Perrin's for the wood... you'll know again what to do with a brush and a trowel?"

The birds were still making a mighty noise up there at the edge of the sky.

"We'll give the fish a break for a little bit. They deserve it. And it will be nice to do another job for awhile... Listen, I'll go see at the quarry... And you can take the fish to the station... I'll be back by noon."

He was still speaking when he turned toward the upper air where the bird song was coming from. Up there it looked like the edge of the sky was being continually lifted up, then it fell back down; it was raised up over the wood like the lid of a saucepan. Rouge hears the shed door squeak behind him again, then the noise from Décosterd's wheelbarrow; it jumped from one stone to another with the sound of a little drum. As for Rouge, he was very happy; which is why, having folded the paper with the map and having slipped it into his pocket, he doesn't rush off. He went into the reeds. First we could see his shoulders and his head, and then we could only see his head. Eventually, when Rouge reached the boats, his cap also disappeared behind the high silvery plumes. On his right the other shoreline rose up in a steep slope, while the one he walked along was low and nothing but a hillside covered in alders where there was a path the fish warden used (and which the trout fisherman, with or without a permit, used as well). Rouge didn't hurry, was this because the weather was so nice? Nor did he take the shortest route (nor perhaps did he need to go himself that morning to the gravel yard; but it was doubtless because of the good weather, because he really seemed to be so happy; he kept on looking happy among the bees, among the white and yellow butterflies, the high stalks of the wild celery, beneath the alders with their black leaves covered in a kind of glue, which made a roof over him with blue-glass windows. The path lost its precision from time to time in the thickets, all while beginning to climb, at the same time we could now hear the Bourdonnette make a noise like a train passing over a bridge. And the shoreline where Rouge was walking also started to climb; then there was a kind of little gorge where the water, having narrowed, fell down steps of soft sandstone which around here we call molasse, into the swamps; — after which an abrupt opening gave onto a wide little valley. A broad, sandy, wild place harboring at its top a lovely stone bridge with many arches, the train viaduct; but elsewhere there is nothing but fields with meager grass, besides the quarries on the left. A poor place, little farmed and where hardly anyone lives, because all you can see is a little house half-shoved into the ground on one side, on the left shore: it was the house of a man named Bolomey, hunter and fisherman, and he lived alone.

A train passed over the viaduct. It was a train without smoke.

Now there are electric locomotives which no longer look like locomotives at all, but like simple wagons except they have a trolley, and then these different wagons are hitched in front of the others.

A train passes over the viaduct with a great whoosh of wind and Rouge, watching it pass, thought, "These electric trains go really fast, they work bloody well!"

The train glides past, effortlessly, in a beautiful irresistible movement; all its windows shine for a moment, it's already past, the noise dies; and Rouge says "Now that's progress! And of course they're saving so much coal... "

He puffed on his pipe, and then looked further to the left: up on the hill, two or three men were working the digger behind the sifts, then they raised their pickaxes and the iron shone in the sun above their heads.

Small wagons rolling on a Decauville track were moving from the gravel pit to a red-roofed construction, but before that the quarry lies before you with its neatly cut levels like children's blocks placed one on top of another, and there were lighted plots and others unlit, so it looked like a kind of tilework; tilework with blue tiles and with yellow tiles in the sun that was not yet very high on the horizon.

We push the gravel from one shelf to the one below using the digger. Then we sift it into different sizes, from the finest sand to actual rocks; Rouge considered that it was well situated, it's lovely here, it's well organized and the men seem like professionals; then he sees the man called Ravinet pushing a small wagon at the road edge, he was from Savoy and could be seen having a drink fairly often at Milliquet's; he was wearing a red belt and a fitted black cotton jersey with no sleeves.

Rouge said, "Hey, how's it going? How about the boss, can I see him?"

Walking beside the Savoyard, who kept pushing his wagon, he continued, "Because, you know, we're going to build. Yes, we're turning to construction. I'm going to need bricks, I'm going to need sand. The boss is going to have to get me some cement, too…he could bring all that around one of these days…"

Later on, he went to Perrin's, the boat builder and carpenter—the man was nearly a colleague of Rouge's; and because his workshop faced Milliquet's café, it was a good time to have a drink.

That day Rouge went three times to Milliquet's…

"Yes," he was saying, "It was too small, it was really too small and it wasn't holding together anymore. So Décosterd and I have turned ourselves into masons."

Luckily there was plenty of water; the sand was delivered, the cement was delivered, some bricks; and by the eighth day, the walls had quickly risen, like when you take good care of a plant, and they were already as high as a man, the walls of the newer part, while Rouge was taking care of the older side.

A big iron bucket set beside him was filled three-quarters

of the way up with a lovely reddish-brown color, thick like cream, which smelled strongly of linseed oil; he dipped his brush, which was three or four fingers wide, he went with his brush along the planks, beginning at the top of the planks to avoid drips; and quickly it all looked different, the front side of the shed was already unrecognizable.

Now he attacked the north side, explaining again to people who came to see and meanwhile all around the bucket were large round spots on the stones like when it starts to rain before a storm.

The weather was beautiful, only sometimes it takes a while to see that it's beautiful.

"And don't you think? We'd ended up living in a pigsty and in the dirt…luckily, we got started in time."

He pushed his nail into the wood and peeled off a scale: "It was starting to rot," he was saying to the people who had come, but it was the girl who came next; and he hadn't expected to see her come, not so soon, and, if the truth be told, a little too soon.

His work wasn't finished yet, but it was that he'd have never believed that Milliquet would have let her come; and in fact what caused it was a particular circumstance, that of a phone call in which some men had reserved for a fish fry that very evening. Milliquet, short-handed, had only the girl to ask.

"You'll know how to get there? A kilo of good perches; you'll remember the name?"

She set off on the path; she'd twisted her little feet right away. Her shadow was before her on the smooth stones, her shadow was before her and taller than her on the stones. She looked at these round, flat stones because of their pretty colors: pink ones, red ones, chocolate ones; brighter colors than those in the water and the ones out of the water are paler; blue ones, white ones and shiny ones and even transparent ones: pieces of glass, chips from plates, that the movement of the water had finally softened around the edges. We continue our story in such a way that already here her eyes were shining with all kinds of beautiful painted stones, and then there was only space between the hillside and the water for the path, hedged at the bottom by a stone wall. Two or three children who were younger than seven years old (the others being at school) were playing there on the sand, having hiked their trousers up to mid-thigh, and they went into the water, but it was still cold and the coldness made them cry out. She enjoyed watching the children; she raised her head beneath her beautiful hair. She went now towards the softer part of the shore and it was soft beneath her feet. Her shadow was all blue; nothing else came to break it up on the sand, elsewhere the ground was irregular, where it is twisted and broken up. The trunks of the pine trees were a beautiful red, because the sun was hitting them on the side. One side of the girl's body was lit up. She stood there, one cheek lit up, one shoulder, one of her arms was lit up. The children yelled again; when a wave came they ran backwards and then they ran forward. She went along with her little black satinet dress and her skirt of the same material which was not long enough, and her basket; then the shoreline widened where Rouge's house sat, with the shiny nice cube, the beautiful freshly painted cube of the shed. The front side could be seen from an angle, and beneath its still wet oil it was like a mirror in the sun, while on the back side, in the shadow, we could see a fat man stop perfectly still in the movement he made with his hand from top to bottom, then he seems to hesitate, then he puts his brush into the bucket (while she is still walking forward), and awkwardly, he wipes his fingers on his trousers:

"Miss, it can't be true! It's you... I didn't expect to see you coming here, Miss... No, I wouldn't have believed it; is Milliquet...?"

She didn't answer him. She'd had one thing to ask him, she'd asked him, that was all; so Rouge said, "Fish? Well, no...no perch, no trout, no grayling. Not even any pike. Everything left on the train this morning...as if Milliquet didn't know this..."

And then, because he saw that she had nothing to do but go, that she was getting ready to do just that, he said, "Is it really that much of a rush?"

Then, "If you could wait just a moment, Miss..."

"Oh, I can't..."

"But yes! I'll send Décosterd fast over to Jaunin. He'll surely get what you need over there. Hey! Décosterd..."

Since he's no longer listening to what she's saying, he calls; and already Décosterd comes over with his fingers all gray and stiff with mortar.

"You've got that?" Rouge was saying, "And, you (to Juliette), let me do it, I'll take care of everything...You (to Décosterd), you go right away. A kilo, a good kilo, you understand?"

"Understood."

Décosterd goes to wash his hands, he goes to put his vest over his shirt, he takes off with big steps and doesn't look back.

And then because there was no one left now but her and him, Rouge said, "You've got to sit down, Miss...Oh, cripes," he said. "It's just that we're fixing things up; I don't dare ask you inside. There's too much of a mess. But at least let me take your basket from you."

He took it from her hands, he carried it into the kitchen; but the girl, no, he'd never dare ask her inside. And while

43

he was in the house, she looked again all around her, she looks up on high and she looks down; she sees the water, the sky, the mountains, then the sand and the stones, the reeds, the great cliff; her face changes, she said, "Oh, I love it…"

It was just when Rouge was coming back; she turns to him: "It's like home."

"Home?"

"Like my country."

"Ah," said Rouge. "It looks the same? All the better if it looks the same."

She said, "Are you a fisherman?… I also know how to fish."

Rouge said, "You know how to fish, do you? How did you learn?"

"With my father."

Rouge said, "Listen, you've still got to sit down… And since you know how the work is…"

He came back with a bag; behind the net poles, the shoreline rose into a hill, and on this he spread out his cloth bag. "Seat yourself here, Miss."

She did as he said; he sits down beside her on the remains of some red roof tiles, amidst the pieces of softened glass and old corks and splinters of wood now become as gray as stone, he continues, mentioning his surprise, "It's just that you speak our language really well… you just have a little bit of an accent."

Because she had a strange accent that cut the end of her words off quite uniquely, and her voice was a little hoarse.

"That comes from my mother."

"What language did she speak?"

"Spanish."

"That's what everyone speaks over there?"

44

"Yes," she says. "But my mother is dead. My father is dead, my mother too."

She became quiet again. She had lowered her head. She held her hands together across her knees.

"He was a foreman for the railroads; he came to see me on Sundays. We went fishing together."

It was as if she needed to tell him everything, but it was also maybe that she'd been silent too long.

"He was sick for only eight days..."

She went silent again, and Rouge didn't dare say anything, while she gently shook her head; he didn't even dare look at her, turning his pipe with its lid over and over between his fingers.

"Eight days, and now I'm here. It's all so different...."

She says, "It was all so different."

Looking again about her, while her face changed again, Rouge said, "Oh, well, in any case, you can consider yourself at home here... If anything should happen to you, Miss... And you can see we're actually renovating everything, what a coincidence! Some might even say it's on purpose..."

And while she was getting up, he continues, "Us, we're not the Milliquets..."

But she shrugs her shoulders, and he sees that she's gotten up, he sees her shrug her shoulders, he laughed, he said, "I see we understand each other..." Merrily, he filled his pipe with a finger and a thumb; the fish were jumping all around up from the water, making little white flashes; it's a lovely day, it's an exquisite day.

She stood up, she turns toward the house, "So, you're fixing things up?"

"Yes," says Rouge, "but that's not all. We're not just fixing things up. You see there, we're adding a room."

He raises his hands close up in front of his face, the bright sunshine lit them up lightly on the inside while the smoke rose up through his gray mustache; then he drops his hands, he pulls his pipe from his mouth as it hasn't yet been lit.

"Oh, no, no," he said. "Don't go in. Wait until it's finished…"

He continued, "Let's go look at the boats instead, since you know about them."

They walked along the shore to the path in the reeds where at first they were beside one another, but then there wasn't enough space for two people to walk forward. Behind Rouge's cap, we saw two lovely black shoulders go between the high plumes which rustled against each other next to the path; then they hid the cap, they hid the shoulders, finally they hid the black hair that shines above the ear (this was all while Décosterd had gone on his errand); then we could hear Rouge's voice. "Oh, it's always the same thing! Décosterd forgot to put up the oars."

Another voice, "All the better!"

They had arrived at the lake edge, and, effectively, the oars of the smallest boat were crossed over the bench;

—up there, beneath the high rocky cliff, with its hedges, its colors, its little pine trees, its thorny and thornless plants, with tufts of grass already grown high, some flowers; and overlooking the cliff were the great pines of the forest filled with birds.

"Miss," Rouge was saying. "You're not thinking to… it should have been tarred this winter: it's a real sieve."

But she said, "Oh, that doesn't bother me."

She was laughing; his surprise kept him from moving; she had already jumped in the boat, making the water in the bottom splash up higher than her in the lovely sunshine; she knocked the chain from the buoy.

46

She definitely meant to start rowing. She took up the oars, rowing at first with one hand only in order to turn the boat toward the open water; suddenly, she leaned back with her entire body: so between the reeds we saw the smooth water parted and pushed away backward, in two lines, and then watched it die softly on the shore.

At first he waits a moment where he is; then he begins to walk. It was as if he needed to follow her with his entire body and all of himself, not only with his eyes. He went between the reeds and the water, in the sand mixed with mud that became always softer and gave way more and more beneath his weight; eventually, he had to stop. At the same moment, she had suddenly tacked and disappeared behind the tip of the cliff.

The only thing he could do was go back, he went back.

The only thing he could do was wait for her to come back, he had to wait a fairly long time.

Now she was in a hurry. "My God," she said, putting her shoes back on, "I'm going to get yelled at."

"Don't be afraid, I'll go with you."

She went before Rouge again into the reeds; they saw Décosterd had been back a long time already and, not having found them, had gone back to work.

"Do you have the fish?" Rouge yelled.

And Décosterd: "Yes, the package is in the kitchen," while he kept laying bricks, one on top of the other, fixing a layer of cement between them with the trowel.

Rouge had gone to get the package, had put it in the basket, came back with the basket; he sees that she'd gone ahead.

"Wait a second, don't hurry like that; you've just got to tell Milliquet that I had to fish these perch... No, don't tell him anything, I'll take care of it." Then, "And there he is."

Because Milliquet had just then appeared and was coming to meet them, making signs to them with his arms from afar; but Rouge said, "What's the problem? You're worried… you shouldn't be… come on, come on, calm down, my friend."

He didn't let him speak.

"You can see we're back on time and you should thank us, because we've fished up the fish for your fry. And we wouldn't have done it for someone else, so you can welcome us a bit better than that, what do you say?"

They arrived in front of the café before Milliquet could even open his mouth, but there waiting was Mrs. Milliquet, and when she saw them she went back inside and slammed the door behind her.

The Savoyard was also on the terrace.

VI

It was several days later...

The first to come to the café were some cattle merchants, two or three of these merchants with their long purple shirts, who had ordered some bottles of wine[†]; after which, the biggest of the three, the one with a black mustache, having pushed back his flat-brimmed felt hat, said, "I like that!"

He crosses his arms on the table: this was out on the terrace, it was one of those green-painted tables; the man, he goes completely over it with his two arms in their wide sleeves with the tight-fitted wrist, embroidered in white.

"I like that who brings the drink is the same quality as the drink, and the serving girl the same as who is served."

Three o'clock in the afternoon. It had rained that morning. A light dampness was still rising with a slight mist between the legs of the tables which were splattered with a light film of dirt that was drying and becoming white as it dried.

"I like that, because it's rare."

A little man with a yellow face who was sitting across from the one speaking nodded his head in approval, holding his hands on the top of his cane; the third of these three men was looking over the wall on the lake side of the terrace.

"And it's rare, it's extremely rare...how did he do it, this Milliquet, how did he get his hands on her? We'd never have thought him clever enough..."

[†] The term « vin bouché » is used to signify bottled wine as opposed to a carafe of the house wine, signaling that these men were important customers.

49

Three merchants who were crossing the countryside in a light pitch pine wagon which was attached to a small slender-legged horse that they had hitched in front of the café; the big one said again, "Where is this Milliquet?"

He hit the table with the handle of his whip which he had taken with some difficulty from between his legs.

It wasn't the one they wanted who came, it wasn't Milliquet either; it was the newest serving girl who came, and she does her job which is to come when called for.

The tall man said, "You're too little…"

Truly, she didn't seem to be more than 15 or 16 years old. She caught her feet in her too-long apron.

"What are you doing here, you? You didn't go to school today? Listen," said the man, "If you bring us the boss, you'll get fifty cents."

Milliquet was in the kitchen; he was just saying to Juliette, "You shouldn't discourage the customers…you know well enough I'm not at liberty here…", when the little serving girl came back.

"Sir, they're asking for you."

Milliquet came to the men.

"Congratulations," said the tall man with the black mustache, "Congratulations, Milliquet. That's what I call dedicated service."

There was a bottle in front of him, it was a Bordeaux with a cork and a lovely label with colors drawing a castle with round towers, with a green and white shield, the name of the wine, the date and the year.

"Oh, yes," said Milliquet, "This wine is particularly suited to its bottle…" He was standing at the head of the table, arms hanging, head sideways, but we could see he was pleased. "It's unfortunate I don't have much of it left."

"You've certainly got one more."

Milliquet began to smile, his pained smile that showed his ruined teeth.

"Well," he said, "for you…"

"Only," said the tall one, "a good wine deserves a pretty girl. Where've you got her, tell us, you old fox. And we're your serious customers, and you send us this child, or is it that you want to keep the other one for yourself? Who is she? And where did you get her? Are you going to tell us, or what?"

Because Milliquet suddenly looked severe, and he didn't answer right away and even seemed like he didn't want to answer (a person has his dignity):—then, because these were, as a matter of fact, good customers, and he couldn't make them too unhappy, he said, "It's my niece…"

"Your niece?"

"Yes, my brother's daughter."

He had spoken coldly, with a kind of superiority; then he told the whole story, from Juliette's arrival (even now flattered by the idea that he still had this whole story to tell and that he would have the other benefit of having conducted himself as a good brother).

"Oh," said the tall dark one, "and then maybe she's rich; lucky devil! She comes from America, the country of dollars!"

But Milliquet shook his head; that was entirely another question.

It was a Saturday afternoon around three o'clock, out on the terrace, before it got busy, because usually everyone comes later; and above Milliquet's head, on a branch thicker than a thigh, one of the first leaves was hanging, all wrinkled up, and it looked like a duck's foot.

At that moment, the man with the black mustache raised his fist, "And why not? Why not, after all? Another bottle and your niece…otherwise, we go…how much do we owe you?"

He moved like he was going to take his wallet out of his pocket.

She was forced to come out. So she came out (or came back). And now on the terrace (Milliquet was no longer there):

"Miss, we still have one seat in the wagon; it's all yours…"

The Savoyard was just passing by the terrace, he was passing there for the second time; he stopped, he looked over the wall, he listened, he went away.

"There are four seats in the wagon, there are three of us, we'll take you with us."

It was the tall one speaking.

"We'd have a lovely room for you, a south-facing room with two windows…two windows and a dresser with a mirror…waiting for your answer, here's to your health."

He drank glass after glass.

"You're not drinking with us, Miss?"

So then he began having trouble finding his words, like when a person's embarrassed; the others were no longer speaking; we hear them all get up.

The tall man follows, then we hear, "Too bad, another time then."

And while the little hooves of the horse were hurrying away, grinding on the paving stones, she runs to Milliquet, she hands him the money and a receipt. "Are you happy now?"

Then she said, "That's the right amount?"

Then, still running, she went up into her room;—and just a moment later, the Savoyard came.

What happened next is that the cattle merchants had

hardly disappeared around the bend in the road when the Savoyard had appeared, or reappeared;—and it's because we are drawn into beauty's orbit. Down here on the earth we don't see enough of it. We are greedy about it, we hunger for it; we want to possess it. The Savoyard came back; he went and sat down on the terrace and he ordered a half liter. He drinks his half liter; then he went to buy some cigarettes at the shop, he comes back with his packet and places it on the table in front of him, and then all he had to do was fish them out, lighting each new cigarette with the one he had in his mouth.

This time he wasn't drinking, and Milliquet, worried about his interests, had started hovering about him without making it too obvious.

Then the Savoyard calls, saying, "I'm thirsty. Where is your niece? Yes, your niece. Miss Juliette. Send her to me to take my order."

Milliquet turned his back.

Where could beauty find its place among men, how could she find her place among us?—he had put on his Sunday clothes, he was wearing a checked cap, he had a collar, a tie, a jacket, a vest, a red belt (the same red as his tie); he sees the little serving girl pass by, he calls her.

He took some money out of his vest pocket, and, showing her his hand filled with coins, he says, "Go get her for me; this is for you if she comes…"

"If you think she's going to come like that…" She was laughing at him. "Put your money away, because I don't think she's coming back down…Anyway, if she wanted, there wouldn't be any need for money to bring her down; and if she doesn't…"

The Savoyard left, then he came back around seven or eight o'clock.

Electric lamps were fixed onto planks between the

branches of the plane trees. On fine summer evenings, when the air was soft, customers stayed out happily on the terrace; and all Milliquet had to do was turn on the switch (with the sole inconvenience of gnats, moths, and bugs, not to mention the mosquitoes, but it isn't until much later in the season that they become a problem). That night there were a lot of people on the terrace: Alexis the dragon among others and some of his friends; being out there was like being in a box with glass walls, walls of a dark blue, being out there was like being behind panels of glass through which the lake and the sky were shining softly.

Suddenly, it seemed like the walls exploded away. Instead of panels of blue glass, it was opaque walls of night that fell all around you, hiding the lake, the sky and the mountain, like being on the inside of a house. The electric lamps had just been lit. It was like being in a room beneath the lights, not knowing what was happening outside the room, except when a little wave came with a kind of a sigh; hunh! Like the sound of splitting a log or a baker making his bread; the sound of hitting the ax against the edge of the iron, or raising both hands above the head with the ball of dough.

This little square world with its tables, three walls of night; and, because of the change of scale, it seems to have grown enormously: three walls and five or six tables, and those who were sitting around the tables, Milliquet was coming and going, Marguerite the little serving girl was coming and going, then we see Milliquet speaking to her.

We could see the colors; we could really see people's hands, their shoulders, the tops of heads with their felt hats, a few straw hats, a few caps; there were about twelve or fifteen people; we could see that the Savoyard hadn't yet come back, because he came back later.

It was a little later that the boss had spoken to

Marguerite, and now she was no longer there, this meant that Milliquet had a lot to do, passing continually from the café to the terrace. Marguerite had climbed up those two floors (while we heard Mrs. Milliquet's door open)…

She had knocked. "The boss tells you to come down."

"No."

"And there was also the Savoyard who asked about you. I told him that you didn't want to come…"

Little Marguerite had knocked, she had said quietly, "Miss, it's me." She had gone inside. We could see that the large leather suitcase had been opened and then beyond that, behind the blinds, the wooden shutters were closed. At first little Marguerite stayed standing at the threshold of the door in her black dress with its white spots; suddenly, she said, "Oh, Miss…" She paused, started again, "It's just that there's a whole group downstairs waiting for you…"

She gestured toward the shutters, behind which they could, in fact, hear a sound like two stones hitting together. They heard a great laugh, they heard people calling Milliquet, they heard someone hit their fist against the table.

"I'm scared," she continued, "that the boss will come up, because he said if you don't go down, then he would come up…"

Then she forgot what she was saying. "Oh, that's so beautiful! What is it?"

Pointing to the things that had been taken from the suitcase, and spread around the suitcase on the bed, "Those are things from your country?"

But someone was calling up the stairway. And she said quickly, "I'll come up again, Miss…I will tell you what's happening…"

She went back down taking the stairs two at a time and

Mrs. Milliquet's door closed again.

While down on the terrace they are all looking up at the second floor, they were looking up from the terrace through the spaces left between the branches of the plane trees, looking at those two windows that touched just beneath the ridge of the roof. We were looking up there, because we knew she was up there (some of us at least knew this), but we saw that the shutters had been closed. Marguerite had just come back down. And Milliquet was going to talk to her when he was called by his wife, a call which Marguerite hears and then Marguerite hears a discussion on the stairs; but still nothing moves up there, while Marguerite had come back to the terrace where she sees the Savoyard in his corner turn his shiny eyes toward her beneath the brim of his cap. The Savoyard signals to her that he has nothing to drink, then he leans on his elbows without a word and puts his hands beneath his chin. It must have been about 10 o'clock.

She asked him, "What would you like?" He hadn't answered her.

She chooses at random, bringing him three deciliters of *petit vieux*; and she was running back into the café when someone grabbed her arm; it was Milliquet, his face haggard (at the same time on the first floor a door slammed).

"Hurry and go serve, and then listen up: this time, if she doesn't come down, tell her that I'm coming up...If she isn't down in five minutes. And that this time it won't be like the others."

He had pulled her into a corner and was speaking close to her face with a finger in the air, "Doesn't matter if she locks the door; I'll break down the door. I'll shame her in front of everyone."

Marguerite had raced back upstairs.

Again, she'd made a little mouse scratching sound against the door panel with her nails; she said, "Miss, can I come in?" The key turns in the lock. "Miss! Miss! He's going to come up! He told me he's giving you five minutes."

She was quiet.

"Miss, Miss," she starts again, "Believe me, it would be best if you would lie down, I'll tell him that you're sick; maybe he wouldn't dare…"

She was quiet again.

And then, "Oh, that's so beautiful! Is it yours? And it comes from your country? What is it? A comb? And these little red balls, they're coral? What is this comb made out of? Oh! It's gilded copper…"

She stuck her hand forward, then brought it back each time against her body; then we see her with her hands crossed over her too-long apron, her eyes shining, looking like a little girl and an old woman at the same time, in the midst of this great silence that has grown;—Juliette stayed with her back toward her, Juliette stood all this time in front of her mirror:

"Oh, those are strange earrings, are you going to put them on? Oh, yes, put them on!"

The room had only a poor little mirror with a metal frame painted in fake wood; there was no other light but the one from the ceiling; the mirror was between the two windows; she had to lean over her dressing table and had to put her face up against the glass; no matter, she leaned anyway, she leaned over with her fingers to her lips, she leaned over with the powder puff to her cheeks.

"Where I come from, a woman makes herself beautiful in the evening. Tonight you will see how the women in my country are dressed. In just a moment…"

But at the same instant the accordion music could be heard.

It was hard for all the noise on the terrace to sustain itself, the high little notes pierced through it everywhere. We had heard them begin in the distance, they came quickly closer.

"It's him! It's him! Oh, I was sure he would come. I don't know what made me believe it, but I was sure…"

She takes the powder puff, she passes it over her face; she says to Marguerite, "Now, give me the comb," while she raised her arms. Oh, it's that she's completely transformed and we can't even recognize her;—tying her long hair up against her neck, she says, "Can you give me the shawl, the long one with the flowers…"

"Oh, Miss, are you going down?"

"Of course, since there's music."

"And your uncle?"

Juliette bursts out laughing.

The accordion was just beneath the windows.

"Because I just knew," Juliette was saying, "that he would come, so I've got to hurry; quick, Marguerite, please, the comb…And then the shawl, just like in my country…"

And then on the terrace, all the voices quieted one by one; everything became quiet, the wind quieted, even the waves quieted; there was nothing but this lovely dance tune which started to turn on itself all alone. It stopped as well, just a moment, and none of us breathed; then, again, those great chords burst forth one after another…

But at that instant, a table fell; and then a voice: "Stop him! Stop him! He's getting crazy…"

And suddenly the accordion was also silenced.

The Savoyard had told the other workers, "I'm not working today…Tell the boss he shouldn't count on me."

The other workers had left as they did every morning for the gravel quarry; the man, having gone to wash himself at the fountain, had shaved; then he'd taken his Sunday clothes from his closet, a clean shirt, a collar, a tie. This was in a house near the station where he and the other workers were lodgers; there, he got dressed slowly. He had a brand new suit, a jacket that fitted at the waist; he had also tried to part his hair, but his hair was much too curly and tangled, so he shoved his cap upon his head, and turning the bill to the front, he brought the hair forward onto his forehead where it stuck out from the bill.

He was smoking cigarettes. He opened the window. Through the window, he asked the woman who owned the house if he could eat his soup a little earlier than usual. He had eaten his soup, he went out shortly after.

He had crossed the big road. He had gone to lie down beneath a tree not far from the highway where automobiles were always passing by, rolling along with flashes of light glancing off their bonnets and with reflections off their windshields like a flame exiting the barrel of a carbine. The cars barked, they coughed, they gave out long howls like a bored watchdog. They rolled over the tarred highway without kicking up any dust—coughing, whistling, barking, crossing paths or passing one another, disappearing behind a hedge, reappearing: ten, fifteen, twenty,—because he'd taken his watch out and amused himself by counting them. He spit between his knees. Then he gets up and, having followed the road, he reached the Bourdonnette not far from the great stone viaduct on which the trains passed and he started to walk down along it, which brought him to the quarry where his colleagues were just getting to work. He watched them working from below, waving to them, wearing his good Sunday clothes, while up there, on their stair steps, behind the sieves, they were naked to the belt or wearing sleeveless shirts: how different he is today. Hello up there! We could see him. Where's he going like that, this Ravinet?

"Oh," we said, "he's a bit crazy. And there are days when it's best not to pay him any mind, otherwise things can go badly." So they raised their arms, or started again to push the blade of the shovel along the top of the soil beneath the heaps of little stones and sand, while Ravinet went away and he was going down along the Bourdonnette, where, beneath the alders, he sees Bolomey the fisherman with his plastic boots. Bolomey was going up along the Bourdonnette. The two men passed not far from one another without saying a word. Here we arrive at the place where the banks are close together, and there, the volume of the water is restricted, it grows deeper, making stairstep waterfalls that the trout go up with a flick of their tail; which is why Bolomey preferred to fish upstream, with his high plastic boots and his flat basket hanging down his back on a strap;—well, now, I couldn't care less about fishing; these fishermen annoy me. He was smoking cigarettes, his hands in his pockets. The water made a drumming noise as it gave way to its forward movement. And then, a little further on, the water becomes all quiet and smooth as it widens: that's where the reeds start, and there are little islands of gravel invading into the middle of the reed bed. Here, Ravinet turned right.

Just then Perrin the carpenter arrived in front of Rouge's house with a load of beams. Ravinet walked up, gradually slowing his steps as if he were wary. He sees this new construction, this new addition that Rouge has done to his building: "Ah, he's building," he says to himself; why is this man building?" And "this man" was Rouge, whom we could see was busy measuring the already unloaded wood with a pocket ruler, all the while looking at his notebook;

he didn't see the Savoyard; it was only the sound of feet on the stones that made him raise his head.

The Savoyard had stopped, his cigarette in the corner of his mouth.

He said, "You're building, are you?"

"Pretty obvious, isn't it?" said Rouge.

"It's for you?" The Savoyard began to chuckle strangely and Rouge, who was surprised, couldn't find anything to say at first.

Then, "Hey now! Is it any of your business? Why don't you bother with your own affairs?"

Only Ravinet, having spit once again, had already walked away and showed only his back to Rouge;—and so he kept walking along the shoreline and arrived in front of Milliquet's pretending it was by chance, then he looked to go in, but he saw the three cattle merchants over the wall.

He went and walked around the village, and then came back a moment later.

Again, he didn't go in. And where can beauty find a place among us when it is so doggedly pursued? Because he went in finally, remember, he sat himself down on the terrace and he ordered a half-carafe which Milliquet brought out to him.

He drank his half-carafe.

He went and bought cigarettes at the store, he came back with his packet and placed it on the table in front of him, and then he said to Milliquet, "Where's your niece?"

Milliquet turned his back.

"So it's like that, is it?"

And he said to the little serving girl, "Go get her for me!" But the little serving girl only laughed at him. "So it's like that, is it?" And he left to go drinking in the café next to the train station.

***

Voices could be heard beneath the window:

"I saw that he'd opened his knife. I'd been watching him for awhile…but what was anyone to do? No one could know, a person can always have something to cut, a long nail maybe, a wart, a shoelace…"

"Of course."

"Remember though that it wasn't really the man he was after, but the instrument. The Savoyard didn't touch the man…"

"Oh, well…"

"No, I'm telling you, he didn't touch him."

"Because we didn't let him. Luckily, Alexis was there…"

She is listening, up there in her room. There was nothing but these voices out on the terrace.

She listens again; there was also a voice inside the house, this other voice, always the same, monotonous, without inflection, continual, unquietable, like when a faucet is left to drip:

"And aren't you happy now? Ah! You've certainly done well, haven't you? Why don't you congratulate yourself? Idiot! You've got what you were looking for! Now they are killing each other in your restaurant, that'll give you a great reputation…Weren't you proud and telling me, 'A hundred francs today,' and then, 'A hundred and twenty francs!' You idiot, because tomorrow it will be zero francs and, if this continues, zero francs again the day after tomorrow… That wanderer, that street girl, that I-don't-know-what, that I-don't-dare-say-what-she-is…"

And a person had to run away from this voice, out onto the stairs, but the voice followed all the same.

Behind the window, she is still listening.

"Oh, there's nothing to be worried about," they were saying on the veranda. "Big Alexis is watching him. There are three or four guys with an eye on things. He won't make another move."

Just then a door closed, Mrs. Milliquet's voice quieted; Juliette sees that no one is bothering about her anymore. Little Marguerite had gone downstairs when the fight started, leaving her alone; no one will see her leave. And too bad if someone stops her, she will fight, she will go out anyway.

No one saw her.

She slides along the little street, like the time before; she climbed onto the wall of the terrace. And when he saw her come in, he only raised his head in greeting as he was seated before the workbench, his accordion on his knees.

We saw that the knife slash had cut across the bellows, in such a way that the rip went from fold to fold; delicately, like a surgeon feeling along the edge of a wound, he brought the two edges together.

He shook his head. Had he really seen her come in?

Then it seems that he did, because he said, "There is no place for me here."

Then he said quickly, "Nor for you."

She wanted to say something. She stepped toward him, but he signaled for her to keep quiet, as you do when there is someone terribly ill in a room.

"So," Rouge was saying, "that night (he should have said tonight because it was only just after midnight), I had been in bed for awhile when I hear the sound of footsteps outside. At first I thought it might be some lovers out, because they don't usually bother about me when they're a little late getting back from a couple's walk in the forest. I hadn't been to Milliquet's because Perrin had brought the wood over and, since it was June, Décosterd and I were able to work at the carpentry until nearly 10 o'clock; we had to use some boards to close up the hole we'd made in the wall of the kitchen...where was I? Oh, yes, I'd fallen asleep. And then I heard a footstep and then a second one, one kind of a step and then another kind of a step, which is why I thought there were two people, when suddenly someone knocked on the door. I said, "Who is it?" and no one answered right away. I had time to get up, put on my trousers and go into the kitchen, because you can't get into the house except through the kitchen and when I got into the kitchen I heard behind the door:

"Is that you, Mr. Rouge?"

"Of course it's me."

"Mr. Rouge, can you open up?"

I was pretty sure I recognized the voice. There was a bright moon and I saw that it was who I thought—Maurice Busset, young Maurice Busset, you know, the mayor's son, and I see that he's holding a big leather suitcase in his hand, while behind him was standing someone who looked like she was trying to hide herself. But really, that girl, can she hide herself? And her shawl was shiny, her silk shawl, you understand, shining on her shoulder.

I say, "What are you all doing here?"

"Oh, Mr. Rouge," says Maurice. "Can't we come in? I'll explain everything..."

I say, "Wait, I'll turn on the light."

I say, "Wait, I'll lock the door."

And then little Maurice told me all that had happened. He asked me if she couldn't spend the night and then stay with me for a few days. What was I supposed to do? I said,

"Of course, only look…it's too bad, Miss, you're just a few days early…" There was a pile of plaster debris in the corner of the kitchen and the hole we'd made in the wall was badly boarded up. "It's too bad!"

She still hadn't said a word. It was only a few days later that I learned the whole story, the story of the Savoyard, the story of the accordion, and all that happened to her…And you know, she was afraid for the hunchback…and it happened while she was at the hunchback's place. And it was Milliquet's wife. The girl, she told me that she'd heard eleven o'clock ring out (and she knew it was the curfew), but when she arrived back at the café there was only her suitcase. Mrs. Milliquet had put it before the door, with all of her things inside. She went all around the house but all the lights were off. And of course she didn't call out…She told me that she thought immediately of me; the only problem was the suitcase, because it was so heavy. This is when Maurice Busset showed up. How he was there, that's another question, but okay, he was there…I said to Juliette, "You'll just stay here. Don't worry about a thing, make yourself at home. Since they've kicked you out…" Oh, I forgot to tell you that luckily I had two mattresses. I only had to lie down on the older one in the kitchen…"

VII

The next morning, Décosterd saw that Rouge was coming to meet him, something that had never happened before in the ten years the two men had been working together.

Décosterd had a room in the village; and every morning at dawn for ten years he arrived to find Rouge in the midst of making coffee that the two men would drink while eating a little something, after which they would head out for fishing.

They stepped into the boat on water that was like washing water. Often, they would have to put their hands up right in front of their faces just to be able to see them. Often, they couldn't see each other, nor the lights on the buoys that marked where they had put the nets. Sometimes they went to the west, sometimes toward the high mountains where the sun rose, towards Jerusalem. In the fog or in the gray air, which became yellow and then pink, in the spring, in the summer, in the autumn, in the winter, for the last ten years, each of them holding a pair of oars,—and every morning when Décosterd would arrive, he would find Rouge in front of the gas stove, something which simplifies a household for a woman because it lights on the first try and all a person needs to do is turn the dial and it turns off.

And yet, that morning, Décosterd saw Rouge coming to meet him and from far Rouge gave him a little sign to stop walking.

First, Décosterd thought there had been an accident. But he saw quickly that he had guessed incorrectly.

Rouge was hunting around for what to say, looking embarrassed. Décosterd let Rouge find his words, something which didn't happen right away, nor without difficulty; the two men were walking now next to one another, hands in their pockets, along the shore; Rouge wasn't walking fast, and he kept slowing down; finally, he stopped:

"Listen, Décosterd, I wanted to tell you...We're not going to be able to go fishing this morning. We can't...we can't leave her alone."

He had stopped completely and Décosterd also, along the same shore that ended at the water with a width of sand on which one can walk without leaving any tracks. And even though they were still a good hundred meters from the house, he kept his voice down.

"It's Juliette, Milliquet's niece. She came last night."

"Oh!"

"That's right, Milliquet's wife threw her out. She's going to stay here."

"Oh!"

Silence.

And then there was again a long moment of silence, after which Rouge started up again (and he was increasingly embarrassed and hesitant):

"Hey, Décosterd, you don't happen to know if the bakery is already open? You could always try to go to the back door...because we're going to need some fresh bread."

"And the dairy, you could stop by; pick up a half-pound of butter...we don't have any more."

"Okay."

"While you do that, I'll make the coffee."

"So, bread and butter?" said Décosterd.

"Bread and butter."

And then Rouge's entire face brightens; and Décosterd says, "Bread and butter and that's all?"

"Bread and butter and that's all." But then he got ahold of himself, "Wait, I'm forgetting to give you money…"

He had opened his wallet, and his entire big face continued to be lit up, even though he had his back to the sun which hadn't yet quite risen up from behind the great line of mountains, a place where it must climb slowly among the rocks on its hands and knees.

Décosterd had already left, in his sleeved vest with its glazed cotton back which was starting to shine, all leaning forward, with his arms which were too long and his long skinny legs; as for Rouge, he had turned back around on his tip toes. He could have been in slippers, his weight alone was enough to make noise on the stones; which is why he didn't move one foot until he was sure the other had found its spot. He goes into the kitchen; he listens, all was silent.

He wondered whether he should make the coffee right away or wait until she had woken up? He calculated, telling himself that Décosterd would be back in twenty minutes, a half-hour at most, and maybe he should wait until he came back…

He hadn't dared sit down, afraid to make noise by pulling the bench out from under the table. He strikes a match to light the stove, then puts it out without having put the fire to the wick.

He goes outside again.

He goes out to see whether he could see Décosterd, even if it was impossible that Décosterd could already be coming back; he went to the water, his head turned toward the village.

68

Small waves were coming, one after the other, to throw themselves down at his feet like a dog that recognizes its master.

He was watching toward where Décosterd should be coming from, but he didn't dare look at the lone window without shutters and where each night, using a ring and nail in the wall, he drew across a kind of curtain made out of thick cloth.

He turned his back to the window and he stayed there, while before him and at his feet the little waves stretched themselves out, their paws forward, their white claws opening out onto the sand. He was fat and short; one side of him, in his blue sweater and his pants, was painted all yellow. He looked toward the village from time to time: and when he did this his neck and the base of his hair turned another color beneath his cap, and the whole time he didn't think to light his pipe. And then, above him, the air was separated into two parts; a part of the sky was silent, but the other made a great noise: it was towards the east, beneath the cliff, because the birds never wanted to be silent, the robins, chickadees, goldfinches, warblers, the blackbird, and they couldn't keep quiet that morning, even though the summer was well underway. Rouge was thinking, "What's the matter with them?" He was annoyed. Just for us, well, they don't bother us because we're up at the same time and even sometimes before them in this line of work, but he was thinking that they would wake her up. He wanted to make them quiet down. And Rouge was hit with both the light and the sound at the same time, while it seemed that the air was trembling with little bursts around our head like when a boiler warms up, or when someone shakes a pile of plates;—then suddenly the blackbird was the only one singing.

It was while the blackbird was singing. He turns around,

"What? It's you, Miss..."

He stops. She laughs. At whom then is she laughing, or at what? While he stood half-turned toward her. He'd only turned his head toward her, with the top of his fat body and his arms which were too short and hanging down.

And so he wanted to speak, but he couldn't find the words. He looks at her, that's all a person is able to do. He looked at her hair; it was so shiny she had what looked like knife glints in her hair. He looked at her neck, her eyes, her cheeks; there was nowhere to stop looking, because there was still her mouth and her forehead...He had to make a great effort:

"Did you...did you sleep well?"

But he saw she was no longer listening. He took two or three steps in her direction; she didn't even seem to see that he was there. She held herself upright, looking to the east, there where the big mountains rise. There, between two peaks was a kind of indentation, like a nest; that was where the sun had just begun to show itself. It looked almost like it was batting its wings. A kind of pink down, lots of tiny pink clouds had begun to climb into the air above it;—like when a rooster keels back onto its hind legs, opening its wings to show off their shine, then he brings them back to his sides, and little feathers fly away,—an abundance of little pink clouds, slipping slowly into the sky, while on the last snow fields the light had hit, like the sheets of tinfoil that children smooth flat with their fingers.

She didn't see Rouge come up; he speaks to her, but she doesn't hear him speaking.

"Excuse me, Miss...I need to get breakfast ready."

But she hadn't heard, because up above the cliffs there was this birdsong that never quiets; all the birds together and then the blackbird; and then another wave higher than the others rose up and came further along the sand. Rouge went into the kitchen; we heard the sound of a pan, into which he'd just poured a bottle of milk. She looked over her shoulder, she looked again at the lake; another wave was born, a second wave that stretched itself out to her before falling onto itself, like a cat. Now Rouge pours the milk into its container, having taken by the handle the brown pot with a bouquet of flowers painted on the side; it's morning, she puffs out her chest, she breathes slowly because the air is so fresh, like cool water; and now Décosterd arrives.

Rouge had just put the match under the milk.

This is when Décosterd arrives and passes by, looking at Juliette without saying anything; under one of his arms was the loaf, in the other hand—held like a book—was the half-pound of butter wrapped in white paper.

"Oh, it's you…now you've got to hurry. Take the cups…"

Rouge forgot that she could hear them.

"Oh, no, we don't even have a tablecloth."

"Of course we don't."

"We'll have to buy one…and try to find a clean plate for the butter."

The same day, he went to Perrin to ask him to come and lay the roof; he had already gone to the shingle shop and ordered shingles; lastly, he'd gone to Milliquet, planning to sort out Juliette's situation as quickly as possible, something that maybe wouldn't be easy.

Because do we know what to do with beauty among men?

Already that morning, when Décosterd arrived at the milk co-op—just after the time when the farm hands stand up off of the one-legged milking stools they belt around themselves, then they unbelt the stool and put the heavy steel milk can onto their backs—they had laughed hard at the sight of Décosterd while they stood with their notebooks around the milk scale.

"So you're to be the maid, Décosterd!"

The room smelled acidic enough to make your eyes water; depending how you move about, the red copper or yellow copper tools throw a bar of light into your face from the sun coming in at the door; and it was clear that everyone knew the story, which is why they were laughing. Décosterd didn't open his mouth.

He asked for his half-pound of butter, that was all; only the owner made a point not to serve him right away, and Décosterd had to wait a long time among the jokes and the cigarette smoke from the young men or the pipe smoke from the old men.

"He's not so stupid, your boss."

"He damned well isn't."

"And so now you're in charge of the shopping?"

Even if Décosterd kept his silence, it was clear that the situation would not be as simple or as clear as we thought.

There was no one in the cafe when Rouge arrived; it was close to three o'clock. The posters from the winemakers, and those with a barrel and gold or silver medals (bronze medals are rarely shown off) were hanging tiredly on the wallpaper in their frames or from their strings passed through brass eyelets.

The little serving girl let Rouge inside; she immediately asked him, "Is it true what everyone is saying? Is it true she's staying with you? So much the better!"

And Rouge wasn't very happy with this kind of question, and he would have preferred not to answer so he sat down in his usual spot, but the girl continued, "And please tell her for me, will you, that I couldn't help her last night. I'd wanted to. I would have liked to come downstairs and help her, but there was no way."

"Is Milliquet here?"

"And I couldn't have even called through the window, she wouldn't have heard…"

But Rouge went on, "And Milliquet…"

"Oh, he's just come home…and you didn't see all those beautiful things in her suitcase?"

"He's just come home from where?"

"He went to get the doctor for his wife."

"What's wrong with her?"

"I don't know. I think her heart isn't so good…"

"Couldn't you tell him that I'm here?"

But right then Milliquet came in.

He stayed standing in front of the door with his awful face, his hands crossed behind his back, then, having made a sign to Marguerite to go away, he said, "Well, well. You're brave, aren't you?"

"Brave?"

"And, in the event that there's a funeral here, you'll remember what I said and what I'm saying to you now. It's your fault…Yes, your fault. Who brought this stuck-up girl to us? Who said to me, 'A brother is a brother'? A brother I hadn't seen in thirty years! That's a brother? And my God, her, a niece! But you wanted her to come, yes, you. You wanted her to come, Rouge, you hear me. And now my poor wife sick…"

"Listen here, listen here…" said Rouge. He was speaking all careful and soft, seated on the other side of the table. "I don't even recognize you. You've switched sides…and just when I came to talk to you about it. Because, so you know, she's at my place, and she's going to stay at my place..."

"You can keep her!" said Milliquet. That's what he said first, then he continued, "Ten to twelve francs worth of breakages last night, without even counting the trouble I could have had with the law. Oh, you can keep her, if it makes you happy. For the kind of customer she brought in..." He was getting angry. But at the same time, he looked around him, and seeing that there was no one in the restaurant and that all was silent, he changed a little, and then he changed even more...

"Okay, what I think is...it's not my business. My wife put the girl out. The way I see it, she's been saved..."

He continued, "And since I'm her legal guardian and she won't be an adult until next year..."

"Wait a second, Milliquet." Rouge began to be afraid. "You just said you were happy to be rid of her. You're contradicting yourself. But, okay, listen, we can work something out. I'm 62 years old, I'm old enough to be her grandfather. And I'll keep her, but you, on your side, as her guardian, it needs to be understood that you put her to live with me, okay? You'll write something down for me."

But the other man didn't want to work anything out.

"We'll see about that," he said. "Right now, I've got something else to do...It's my poor wife. Her heart is ailing her. As for the girl, if we need to we can put her in an institution."

"You're crazy," said Rouge. "Listen, it's understood that I'll be paying her wages. And since she's a minor, you'll get the money. How much do you want? Thirty francs, forty francs?"

"Nothing," said Milliquet.

And the subject was re-discussed once more, because Milliquet said, "In any case, I've got her papers. She can't do anything without me...and do you think I'm going to take money from an old customer like you? What would that look like? And since I'm leaving her with you for now. I can't say it any clearer, however."

They were still the only two in the restaurant, which meant that Rouge didn't have a witness to call on if the need arose; he had no witness, nor paper, something he couldn't help seeing once the conversation had finished, he said to himself, "I'm here, and I've got my tongue."

To reassure himself, "And then, as long as no one does anything, not Milliquet and not the authorities. And I'll just have to watch Milliquet...as for the authorities, they know just how to...."

He'd now reassured himself completely and he walked home; he was in a hurry to get there.

The worn stones became boiling hot beneath the soles of his shoes.

In the low wall of the new part of the house, he saw Perrin handing fresh butter-colored chevrons up to Décosterd who was standing beneath the already-set crossbeams; pieces of dishes, shards of glass were farther forward, with their little fires like lit candles; the sand along the lake edge was one color, because it was wet, and then it was another color.

Rouge came up looking all around, then he began looking hard as if something was missing; then he walked faster, and from far he yelled to Décosterd, "And...and Miss Juliette?"

"Oh, she left a long time ago."

"What did you say?"

"Yep, she left with the boat; I gave her the oars..." They always took in the oars from the two boats once they'd finished with them, just to be sure, on account of any easyminded walkers who might have liked to take a little tour on the lake. "She asked me for the oars, and I thought it a good idea to give them to her…"

We saw Rouge pass close to the two men. The sun lit the cliff from the front. The sun had turned in the sky and was dropping, its light already hanging low in its arc against the west wall, from there it hit the gravel quarry making shapes like little sponges. These shapes lay flat above you between the prickly hedges and thornless scrubs, some low oaks, dry terrain plants with sparse greenery and high stalks, sweet clover, wild carnations or horsetails. The sun hung above Rouge like some sort of large reflector, while he eagerly pushed aside the reeds, and he was saying to himself, "She's lost her mind!" He saw that she had selected the smallest and oldest of the two boats (like the other time). The *Coquette* was painted green; the inside was yellow. "A boat that takes water like a sieve…" Suddenly, he looks out at the wide lake, then we see that he took off his hat and was shaking it in wide circles above his head…

She didn't see Rouge right away. She was looking over the edge of the boat into the lake depths. There were fish there, as long as an arm, resting flat in the still water; you could see them open their mouths. Every once in a while, they moved a little, they turned a little, like on an axis; she saw them open their mouths and a big cluster of bubbles stuck together rose up through the thickness, from deep to shallow, toward her. Like a peddler releasing balloons, only these weren't red,—she leaned forward even further.

"Miss, Miss Juliette!"

She sees a head, then a cap above the reeds, then Rouge entirely, coming forward from the side of his house;— she just had to flick the oar.

A single flick of the right oar, then go backward with

both shoulders and once with her entire body, then once again, and her momentum brought her where she needed to be.

He waits on the shore; he steps out onto the little mooring, he gives her a hand to get out of the boat (there were two moorings made from a few pylons and old boat planking); he holds out his hand, he kept his eyes lowered.

And quickly he started up, "You didn't see? Just another moment…"

"And then what?" she said, "As if I don't know how to swim!"

He pulled on the boat's rope, he said, "It doesn't matter. Don't use it again until I've fixed it. We'll get it ready right away. Perrin is even here right now, he'll help us. With three, it will be easy…"

He turned his back to her while speaking, looking very busy with bringing the boat to himself; as for her, she had raised her arms to her hair and there was a kind of sunfroth along their edges and at her neck; her too-tight corsage had split at the stitches.

He doesn't look at her. He put his hands around his mouth to make a kind of megaphone. "Hey, over there…" And over the reeds again, "Hey, over there, Décosterd…"

A voice comes back, "Eh?"

"Come on then, you and Perrin."

He was saying, "It's just that these boats are so hard to maneuver, but once it's time to do the thing…" The two men arrived, he said, "Give me a hand, now…"

They were a little surprised but they carried the boat, the three of them, up to the house.

We saw that everything was being done at once; the shingles had arrived. They put the *Coquette* on its back onto two sawhorses, the keel in the air. Everything had to happen at once because just after Rouge said, "the *Coquette*, that's a name that doesn't mean anything, you see it everywhere…"

Now he was scraping the old paint from the boat with a knife, and the color disappeared, leaving the wood undressed. He started again, "And once we've done it, we'll give it a new name…If, of course, you agree, Miss Juliette, and, if that's the case, you'll be its owner…we'll call it the *Juliette*. Okay? Perfect, that's what we'll do, we'll give it your name. It's a lovely name."

The dust of such good weather was floating everywhere along the horizon. Just like harvest time and the same brown dust rises on the roads and in front of the barns. The sun was completely red; its outlines were so pure it seemed to have been cut from a box with scissors (it was perfectly round). We could stare at it.

Rouge was scraping the boat. A little fire was lit on the shoreline.

VIII

That Sunday morning around 11 am, little Emilie arrived in front of the Busset's great pink house wearing her best dress. A terrace stretched forward from one side of the courtyard. On the ground floor was a room for the maid, then a storage shed and further off were the stables and the barn; to get to the first floor one had to cross the terrace to a stone stairway with an iron railing that stood in the shade of a great unpruned plane tree. Usually, before, Emilie went straight up, but that day she stayed in the courtyard. She looks toward the windows. She stays on the little square of pavement which had been well-swept the night before and where the broom prints were showing in the dirt around. She looks toward the windows, toward the barn, toward the shed; toward the high round door of the barn which is closed, toward the shed with its square door, toward the stable with its braided straw over the door. No one could be seen anywhere. Usually, before, she went straight up to the first floor and surely she would find someone because it was soon time for the noon meal, but she didn't dare. She held her black hymnal in her left hand, and, from beneath her blue-ribboned hat, she only raises her eyes, just in case someone would come along by chance, just in case maybe someone had seen her and was coming down.

But we weren't coming, no one was coming.

After a moment she left. She walked back up the street which changed slowly as it went along, crossing paths with people who said hello to her and she said hello to them without looking at them, her head down, her eyes hidden (luckily) by the brim of her hat. She walked up the street to the end of the village; once there, she turned and walked back the way she came.

She was wearing a pretty white scarf dress dotted with bouquets of blue flowers, a cloth collar. She held her hymnal in her left hand, she had white cotton gloves. She had made herself pretty for him. She was only seventeen years old; he was eighteen. A girl washes her hair in a basin filled with chamomile shampoo, just before going to sleep; a girl rolls the tendrils carefully in leather strips; and in the morning, once the sun is up, she can see the lovely honey color they have—and all this is useless, and all these things are for nothing.

And your pretty dress shoes the color of hazelnuts, the same, and your white silk stockings, and everything, and even if a girl is rosy and fresh, and the lovely cheeks she has or that she had—that a girl could have again if only he wanted.

But he didn't want, she was sure, and so she walked back the way she came. And just as she was about to arrive before the house again she saw three of her friends coming up the street, the street that led down to the lake and at the other end of which was the Café Milliquet. The girls were walking and holding hands; from afar they waved to Emilie.

"Oh, luckily we found you... What are you doing this afternoon?"

"I don't know."

"So we can count on you. Mathilde has invited us. She told us to stop by and get you, but we thought perhaps you already had plans... besides, you know, you can just bring Maurice..."

She said, "Thank you. I'll see."

They didn't say anything else. Maurice...

And already they were walking away, talking again, "Well, see you later then..." As for Emilie, she walked on only always more slowly, because maybe he would come; she passes again in front of the courtyard, crossing it, and again she slightly raises her head, but she didn't stop, she didn't have the strength to do it, she would have liked to, but she couldn't.

However, around two o'clock she made up her mind. Weren't they nearly officially engaged, after all? They had known each other forever and who knows when they went from knowing to that other thing. A border line is only marked on a map and in books; it isn't visible in a person's heart. It happens without a person noticing, and all we know after is that it's been crossed; and so now of course she could go over, she even told herself she had to, otherwise Maurice's mother would be surprised.

She found Mrs. Busset on the terrace, "Oh, Emilie!" Mrs. Busset was reading her newspaper, seated on a rushed chair beneath the great plane tree; she took off her glasses. Then she said, "My poor Emilie, you're getting here too late... Maurice has already gone out... Oh, you didn't know... he told me there was a Youth Club meeting this afternoon; it's for the party... You didn't have plans together? Okay, well, sit down... I'm all alone, you can keep me company. Maybe he'll come back earlier than he thought."

But Emilie did not sit down.

Mrs. Busset put her glasses back on and she picked up her newspaper because she already considered Emilie part of the family. Only when she saw that Emilie was still standing she raised her eyes again, looking through her shiny glasses. "You don't want to sit down? You're worried you'll be bored with me? Well, that's normal, you're young. Listen, come back for tea-time, maybe he'll be back..."

Emilie did not answer her. She goes back down the stairs. And she goes... but where to go? A girl exists only where he is; nothing exists where he isn't.

She tries again to walk as far as Café Milliquet, where she tells herself, without believing it, that she'll find him on the terrace.

Only a few people are seated on the terrace; at the ninepins game there are only two or three older men with their pipes and that's all.

Two or three men with their pipes and a piece of chalk, and the blackboard nailed to a tree trunk, and nothing, and emptiness all around;—while we hear the ninepins, crashing one against another, making such a sound like a person bursting into laughter and this gives you a pain in your heart.

All that time Maurice was sitting at the top of the cliff, having slid to that spot, far from any path.

Just below him on the shoreline was Rouge's house; for the moment the house had three colors. The new part of the roof was a light red; the old part of the roof was showing tiles already browned by storms and the sun; and there was also the shed with its tar-papered cardboard roof.

The roof of Rouge's house was tricolored, but the walls, or at least what we could see of them, were everywhere the same lovely deep butter color (like when the cows are fed on grass, which gives the butter a darker color).

This was just about the time when one day Rouge had brought out an iron box from the cupboard and placed it before Juliette and said, "Me, I've never put my money in the bank... It felt like going to steal my own money from them... me, my money, I keep it at home... I'm telling you this, Miss, so you'll know where to get it. You can see it's convenient; no need to write anything down or sell any shares..."

This was after the house had been repainted and, having finished all the exterior work, it was time to work on the inside. He had brought out his box and was saying to Juliette, "Luckily we've got all this money on hand... You see, you've only got to say the word... this money has done enough sleeping in this box... You'll have to tell me what kind of wallpaper you'd like for your room, Miss Juliette. And then of course, we'll have to see about the furniture..."

And he was saying, "What timing! I was making it bigger, I was making it bigger, why was I making it bigger? Old people need less space... I was freshening things up; I was freshening things up, and then at the time... Oh, what timing! Seems like you just had to come... it was meant to be..."

And then, "But for now... this wallpaper..."

"Listen, I'm not sure if I can say..."

"Oh, yes, tell me!"

"Well, where I come from, we don't use wallpaper, we paint our walls white..."

"Understood! Nothing easier than that... It's even cleaner and done more quickly. So, all white?"

"Everything white."

And so Décosterd and Rouge simply whitewashed her room, and she'd helped them, laughing and enjoying the pots all filled with creamy paint and the big brushes. Instead of floorboards, there was a red tile floor; and, when everything was finished, she'd started to dance on it, saying, "It's just like at home."

"Like at home? This is your home now."

"Like home, like home," she sang, turning toward Rouge amidst the strong smell of plaster and glue, but the sun coming in full at the window would have it all dry soon.

And Rouge seemed completely happy, then we could see him looking at a brochure and, since Décosterd was ready to head home at that moment, he said, "Décosterd, I'm counting on you for tomorrow. Be sure to come early. And don't leave at all. You can always put the curtains on the windows, you and Miss Juliette."

He had, in fact, already ordered curtains from the seamstress in the village, but now he had to deal with the furniture, and once Décosterd had left, he said, "So, for the furniture... I would take you with me, but... there's nothing to fear with Décosterd. I prefer you stay here, only you'll have to tell me..."

"Oh, get whatever you like... Back home..."

"What are they like?"

"Well, there's nothing or hardly any..."

"Would you like white furniture?"

"If you want."

"A table," Rouge was saying. "A chair or two... I know just where to go..."

He wrote down the sizes of what they needed. "And then," he said. "I'll buy you a lovely big mirror. It's more important than anything else for women... I'll leave early tomorrow morning, I'll be back in the early afternoon. You'll wait for me here. I prefer," he said, "that you don't go anywhere. I'm a little worried... But as long as Décosterd is here."

He continued, "And now there's just one more question. Which is... Yes, while we're talking about it. All that sleeping money, we could..."

He said, "...have clothes made."

He said, "What I mean to say, if you don't have enough clothing, not enough dresses..."

But she started to laugh, "Dresses! You haven't seen them yet, they're all still in my suitcase. My father always asked me to dress up when he came to town on Sundays and he always brought me a gift… they're dresses from my country."

She was still wearing her little black satinet dress, and he glances at her quickly, then quiets; and then he continued, "Well, so… all right, if by chance I see something that might suit you, since I'll be there…"

And the next morning, he took the train; then, the day after that the entire village was surprised to see a delivery truck, light green with gold letters, turn shakily onto the shoreline and so we followed it.

We could see from afar what came out of it:

"Well, he's certainly rich," we were saying. "There's your proof."

"Goodness! How long has he been working? Forty years. And he's done well, no doubt about it. And he spends nothing…"

While two cap-wearing employees continued to unload huge packages wrapped in gray paper:

"That's got to be a chair, that…"

"And that, that must be a headboard…"

"Yup, there's the other end."

"My God, he's bought her a bed…"

And down below the two employees brought out three or four wrapped boxes from the car, after which, snorting and blowing a thick blue smoke, the car turned around clumsily on the shoreline, the rear wheels slipping halfway down into the water.

That was on Friday, a Friday afternoon. She had been living at Rouge's for a little more than three weeks. On

Saturday morning then, she left with them to go fishing. Rouge made her sit on the rear bench. "Would you know how to direct the rudder, because it would help us if you did..." She knew how. They go out onto the water, in the early morning, all three of them, they head toward the lights of two lanterns sitting in their half-barrels, and that the sunshine had put out, or nearly, making the flames all pale behind the beveled glass. They fish. They had a good catch. They had begun a life, three people together, and it seemed she had her place. Then Décosterd headed to the train station with the crates of fish. And then Rouge went into the shed, inside which there is a scale, several pairs of oars, both new and old, keep nets piled in a corner; and then, anchored to the wall and hanging like garlands, nets that are green, or blue, or green-blue, because they were dipped in sulfate.

He had gone into the shed; he had tied a hemp apron around his body, the kind with a big pocket in the front.

He went out; he goes behind the shed.

He goes to where the poles are and where we hang the nets out to dry, and the ones from that morning were there and still drying, because they have to be dried, otherwise they get moldy. She came too. She saw that he took a shuttle from the apron's big pocket, then went over to those walls of mesh, holding his belly turned toward them, while she watched him work. All these nets started at the side of the shed and went on for about ten meters along the wall, and because they were transparent they seemed to rise up off the ground like a light mist, the kind we see in the morning on the fields when the dawn light is strong. Rouge leaned over beneath his navy blue cap with the visor that sparkled, and, taking up a fistful of mesh links, he let them slip through his fingers. If there are holes, they must be patched right away to keep them from growing any bigger. Holes made in the net by fish that are too big or by waves, or even when the net is raised and gets caught in the cleats; and so each morning the nets must be checked and Rouge was checking, and we saw him, holding the shuttle between his fat fingers, running it along with the tip pointing up, sliding it quickly between the interweaving threads. The fat man lowered his head beneath his cap. He brought the shuttle to him, makes a knot. He made a knot. He took his knife out of the apron pocket, he cut the line with his knife.

It's detail work, delicate; it was one half of the profession, and one which hardly resembled the other half; —he let the links run again through his fingers and the weight at the bottom pulled them down; then he pushed further, the belly of his blue apron always turned toward the transparent wall. Just then he raises his eyes. She was there, watching him work. She had sat down against the hillside; she was holding her hands on her knees. And from his side, he watches her, then he said, "You see, that's how we do it."

He continued, "You want to try?"

She stood up, "Is it hard?"

"Not at all!"

"Would you show me?"

She came over and he said, "Of course. But would you really do it?"

He looks at her, "It's just that it really is a woman's work. The rest of us have to do everything that has to be done, but it's a double-sided profession. We do the man's part, we do the woman's part, because there are no women here or at least there never was a woman here. But now…"

He went to get her another shuttle.

She's taken her place among us, her place was just here

waiting for her. We couldn't have found someone who suited him better.

He came with the second shuttle, then it was the both of them leaning over the net, her black hair and his cap.

The next day they would rest. Rouge had said to Décosterd, "Tomorrow you can come at eight o'clock…"

He'd arranged the whole day with Décosterd, "Tomorrow, rest. We're not going to fish on Sundays anymore. We have to let her sleep, because now, on the other days, she is going to come with us. Eight o'clock at the earliest. Eight o'clock, eight-thirty…"

Décosterd had done what was asked of him. It was close to eight o'clock when Rouge woke up. She was still sleeping. He walked silently in his slippers. He goes to the door and opens it; he sees that the weather is fine. Then he sees Décosterd arriving and we see that Décosterd is holding something in his hand, walking with care, a loaf of bread under his other arm.

"What have you got there?"

Décosterd says, "It's a surprise."

It was a large leaf of Swiss chard, and another leaf covering that one; whatever was between the two leaves couldn't be seen, which is why Décosterd's face scrunched with pleasure, watching Rouge with an eye that shined, something that made his other eye look darker, more dead than ever.

And Rouge hid his curiosity, "Who's it for?"

"Ah!"

Rouge quiets, then he continues suddenly, "Listen, we have to get the table set quickly… And then," he said. "Since it's a surprise, you can put it on her plate."

Décosterd bobbed his head; and, just as they'd said, when she came in, the two chard leaves were at her table setting—when she arrived in her little black dress.

"It's for me? What is it?"

Rouge said, "Goodness, I don't know."

Décosterd said, "Me neither."

"I can look?"

And, lifting the leaf from underneath, settled into the cup of the other shiny leaf, with its white part and ridges, she found the first strawberries of the season, the first wild strawberries.

"From you?" she asked Rouge.

Rouge made a sign that it wasn't him.

"From you?" she said to Décosterd.

He also shook his head no; she shrugged her shoulders.

The door was wide open; the entire beautiful Sunday came in, with its rowboats, with its steamboats. On Sundays people love to come down off the mountain and from the villages up the hill or behind the hill; young people, boys and girls; and it's when this beautiful water starts to shine between your field stakes and it calls to you from the lake over your little walls. People come happily to rent a boat from Perrin for an hour or two. And there are the big steamboats, all white with their red, green and white, or tri-color flags, and their big wheel beating the water, each flat thud can be heard before we even see the boat; or we can even hear singing. Boys' voices or girls' voices singing songs in duple or triple time, and in chorus, and it's hard to tell where the songs come from, because water carries sound and sends it all around. In through the wide open door came the voices along with the reflection of the little waves which came to hit the freshly whitewashed ceiling. We were lit up twice, we were lit from below and from above, while the coffeemaker was shining where it sat on the table. A new steamboat with its name on the side, which they could read (it was the Rhône), had no front nor a back, for just a moment, as it sat between the two sides of the door, while the coffeemaker was shining where it sat on the table. The coffeemaker shone, the cups had several reflections instead of just one. They had just finished eating; with her fingers she picked up her strawberries from the beautiful green leaf. Suddenly, Rouge gets up. The steamboat had passed. Décosterd pushed himself back and the bench scraped on the cement floor. It's a beautiful Sunday. We see Rouge going out, his hands in his pockets, heading to the water like usual. Décosterd had started clearing the table. She had tried to help him, but he'd forbidden her, "No, Miss, that's my job."

So she'd gone back to her room and there too it was shining bright: the bed, the walls, the ceiling, the tiles. There were white curtains on the window. There weren't only two lights in the room, but an entire crisscrossing of light because of the big mirror hanging on the wall. The daylight danced on her hair, moved atop her shoulders. She went in front of the mirror, she had to close her eyes. She goes all the way up to the mirror, rolling a piece of hair between her fingers beneath her ear; and the weather is extremely fine;—so why did, all of a sudden?...

It was while she was there and while Rouge was at the shoreline; she heard him coming and going.

She looks through the curtains; she sees that he also doesn't look like he knows what to do, walking along the lake, his hands in his pockets.

What is wrong? She doesn't know. And people were even singing in a boat on the water; bathers at the foot of the cliff were calling to one another with loud voices, with laughter muffled by the water; she goes out, she went to join Rouge; at that moment the church bells had all started to ring.

We could see, over the forest of pines, the square tower and its roof with the rusted white iron ridges, topped with a red-painted rooster. She came to stand beside Rouge; then he showed her the belltower. Then he showed her other things all around, while the fish jumped at the angle of his shoulder and before his face, along the slope of the water. It's Sunday, everywhere a holiday. The bells are rung, people sing in the water on their boats;—he watched her from the side. We heard the sound of the dishes from the kitchen where Décosterd was putting the house in order; and the two bells rang out in the air again, one with short, fast notes and the other with long deep notes, spread apart.

Suddenly, "Isn't that a pretty sound? It's just that it's Sunday today. Everything makes itself beautiful."

He continued, "Except for you."

He stops speaking, they listened to Sunday. They heard again the singing in the rowboats, the bathers yelling and laughing, calling to each other at the cliff, the last blackbirds; he watches her. And the girl, she looks at herself. She looks at her little black dress, she sees her bare feet in her old leather slippers.

"Oh," she says, "I don't dare. You remember, the other time, I was yelled at so much..."

"Now, I think," he says, "no one would yell at you."

"It's just that it isn't the custom here, and we don't have the same fashions at home..."

"Home?"

"Yes, you know, far away."

And then he said, "Exactly."

"Well, if you like."

She laughed and said, "Well, wait a minute..."

And this was why, looking down from up above, he hadn't recognized her (Maurice up there beneath his shrub),—much later, when she had come out. A great bright yellow color surrounded her now in the sunshine where she came out, then she'd walked forward in the sun.

He hadn't recognized her right away: she had to get all the way to the water. Once there, she turned around like she was speaking with someone.

The front of Rouge's house was at an angle for Maurice and was hidden from his perspective, so much so that he couldn't see to whom she was speaking. But at least he could see her directly, he could see that it was really her and that a floral shawl hung around her body all the way to below her knees.

He sees everything now like seeing through glass lenses; he sees that she is there, that she stands up, then she turns herself around laughing over her shoulder, that she walks backward slowly. Then, the angle of the wall removed her little by little from our eyes, the angle of the wall took her from us.

From beneath his shrub, Maurice watches all this happening: a moment later a little raft appeared. There were two children in the raft; they couldn't sit down, they had to stay standing, their feet in the water up to their ankles, maneuvering a kind of rudder they'd made themselves, and the raft, too, they had made it themselves with two or three planks nailed to a crossbeam over two barrel halves. They were completely naked, and completely tanned, since it had been warm enough for swimming for awhile now, they had nothing but a little blue and white striped swimming suit around their middle.

The raft had just appeared before the pine tree forest; they could be heard yelling and fighting; they were saying, "Ernest, watch yourself, you're tipping the boat…"

"No, you are."

"You are, I tell you!"

And they were still behind the great ray of light that cut the lake in a crossways direction, going from beneath the sun up to the shoreline; just like one of our highways, with the same bumps, the same dips, the same knots (the kind of knots you find in a worn-out board); then they slipped behind this road, which turned them black and their boat, too.

This was all still happening on that Sunday afternoon. Everywhere the people are talking, songs everywhere, and voices and laughter. Maurice sees people walking along the shore, he sees from beneath his shrub that there are still rowboats coming and going, and then further out;—he hears the shouts of the children, he looks for their raft, he burns his eyes trying to find it. For the longest moment, he sees nothing before him but garnet and red and pink circles, circles that grow in size until they fill both holes of his eyes. And, even Juliette, when she reappeared, she was only a smaller yellow spot within a great yellow circle, as if his vision was tricking him, and creating her falsely for him ;—but then the yellow spot moved, she came to life, moved to a different spot; she too, became black, in front of the sparkle on the water...

"Hey, over there," Rouge yelled, "what a bunch of beginners! Why don't you try rowing together?"

Rouge had come forward, Rouge had joined Juliette, then Décosterd, too. At the same time, the raft had moved into the beautiful blue water which made the tan little bodies of the children regain their color.

"Ernest, you row on the right... Louis, put yourself on the left. Further left, Louis, like that..."

This was when she drew up to Rouge. We saw her talking to Rouge; she must have been asking him something. We see her talking to him, then she quieted, tipping her head to

93

the side, then she nodded several times like a person insisting. Finally, Rouge must have said yes. She started clapping her hands together.

Maurice sees Décosterd coming toward him with a long stride, as if Décosterd had discovered his hiding place; but Décosterd didn't raise his head, held it down in fact, his neck stretched forward. He stepped into the reeds.

Maurice followed Décosterd with his eyes for a minute; he draws them back to the shoreline; he sees that she was again gone.

Now Décosterd is unhitching the boat that used to be called the *Coquette* but was no longer called the *Coquette*. The boat had been completely refurbished; it was painted green on the outside and dark yellow on the inside. Décosterd grabbed ahold of the oars. First he rows between the reeds, in the cloudy water: he turns to the right, the clear water welcomes him. He turns toward Rouge's house; he went aground just in front of Rouge, giving a last push of the oar to set the bow, scratching against the sand. Décosterd jumps onto the shore; he waits, Rouge waits. And the *Juliette* seems to be waiting, too, balanced gently on her stomach, her large hips bobbing irregularly beneath the oars stretching flat; waiting, many little fish could be seen shining, jumping out of the water like from a frying pan.

This is when she reappeared; and there was great joy on the mountains. She walked forward, she walked beneath her silk scarf; as she walked forward, we could see the long fringe slide up the length of her legs, then split to fall along each rounded side of them. She placed her lovely bare feet on the stones. And then, suddenly, the yellow shawl was gone,—at the same time Décosterd pushed the *Juliette* into the water, at the same time the mountains shone bright, the fish were jumping out of the water.—but she was shining now too, her bare arms shone, her broad shoulders shone. We could hear the cries of the children on the raft; because she was coming straight to them, in a game. She had taken up the oars, she had directed the tip of the *Juliette* toward them: at first they tried to escape her by rowing, then, seeing that they wouldn't make it, they threw themselves into the water, one after the other.

Up on the mountain, he was still watching. He had seen that at this moment the mountains were touched on their side by the sun dipping down, at the same time the light turned less white; there was a color like honey between the walls of rock. Lower down, on the slope of the fields, it was like powdered gold; above the woods, like warm cinders. Everything was making itself beautiful, everything was making itself more than beautiful, like a rivalry. All these things making themselves more beautiful, always more beautiful, the water, the mountain, the sky, all that is liquid, all that is solid, all that is neither solid nor liquid, but it all holds together; it was like an agreement, a continual exchange from one thing to another thing, and between everything that exists. And around her and because of her—what he is thinking and telling himself up there. There is a place for beauty...

The children were pulling themselves up to their boards with great difficulty, laughing. They yelled something to Juliette, spitting water from their mouths and running their hands through their hair and along their faces;—now we understand what they are saying, "Miss, wait, we'll come and tow you behind us."

What happened next is that she let them do it; they come to her, they pass the rope from the front of the rowboat through the planks on the back of the raft, they leaned on their oars.

She let them do it; she approached slowly, being pulled

and led by the children: she came, she came farther forward;—then suddenly we saw that Chauvy was there with his same dented bowler hat, his big beard, his jacket; we see him walk to the spot on the shore where she was going to land; once there, with a big sweep of his arm, he doffs his cap.

He showed his bald head.

But Rouge runs over to him.

Then Rouge, turning to the other people: "And you, what are you doing here?" And then angrily, "Is this your home? Get out of here, understand?"

All of that same afternoon, while we were playing ninepins at Milliquet's, and between two rolls of the ball, this funny little music was playing.

The entire afternoon, from behind the sheds.

No one paid attention to it because those who were playing ninepins were too busy writing their points on the blackboard.

First there was just the same note, held long, then a silence, then this same little note coming back. Then a silence.

Then another note came.

Little by little, the notes ran up the scale, slowly first, then more quickly, and then even faster, and always more quickly; the notes went up the scale, they went down the scale; they went up the scale and then down the scale like a spray of water that rises and falls at the same time.

The night came: now he was trying the low notes. Then trying them as chords. The bellows stretch wide and the burst of air snores through the reeds. A first chord, a second.

It all required great carefulness. We could hear how lovingly cautious were the movement of the hands.

IX

This was around the same time that people started coming to Milliquet with underhanded smiles; we were saying, "And your niece?" He was standing before you, leaning with both hands on the edge of the table.

People were saying to each other, "You'll see, we're going to make him let go of the edge of the table..."

"And your niece... So, it seems she's doing well?"

And so, in fact, he would take one or two steps backward, he would shrug his shoulders, he would cross his hands behind his back; but, for the moment, we were holding onto him, we weren't letting him escape so quickly.

"Yes," we were saying, "and is it true what they say? You should know. It seems Rouge has put her up with furniture... it seems he's bought her the best furnishings to be had."

So Milliquet would take a few more steps backward, then, just as he stepped through the door: "Oh, not to worry, it won't last long."

"What will you do?"

But he was already outside, and we had to wait for another day to ask him about it again.

This particular Monday, the story of the raft provided the occasion. The story had made some noise around the village. The mothers of the two boys had started it all by stuffing them into bed without supper, one after the other; then the mothers had gone around telling the story to their neighbors.

We were saying, "Well now! We're having a lot of fun at Rouge's, aren't we! It seems now everyone goes swimming all together!"

Milliquet was just pouring them something to drink; he was obliged to finish filling the glasses: but then he crashes the mug down on the table:

"Leave me be, will you? As if I didn't know what I've got to do..."

"What are you going to do?"

"Well...you think it bothers me, but I've got plenty of time."

"What about it? You're in no hurry."

Everyone starts to laugh, we were saying to him, "And after that? Once you've decided?"

"It's simple. I'm lodging a complaint."

"Since you're the one who kicked her out."

"I kicked her out?"

"Your wife, if you prefer... You and your wife, legally, it's all..."

"Have to see about that first..."

"It's all clear, you're responsible...but then what? Lodge a complaint and then what? Then you take her back with you?"

And laughter again, because this was exactly the point, and we were saying to Milliquet, "All in all, you see that you've made a bad deal..." which was true.

The little serving girl knitted for hours on end alone in a corner. The sparrows felt completely at home in the plane trees on the veranda, which they filled with their chattering, spotting the tables with white that burned off the color. And all this time Milliquet, in his dirty shirt and his old slippers, went around dragging his feet up to the doorstep, waiting on the few customers who remained, and at the same time dreading to see them as if they were enemies he might have had; while he still had to avoid his wife, who, unfortunately for him, hadn't been bedridden for very long.

Rouge had not come back.

As for the girl, she'd gone on fishing with us. She'd gone on having a place among us, when she got into the boat, leaving each morning with us to go raise the nets. She held onto the rudder; Rouge telling her, "Right…left…straight on…" she pulled one of the ropes, or the other, seated on the rear bench. In the beautiful weather that lasted all of the rest of that month and for much of the next, they set out together, the three of them, and this space where she found herself, it belongs to us. It seemed she was right where she should have been: look carefully, beneath the mountain, look carefully, among the stones and the sand, or first on this water that is gray, then lemon yellow, then orange yellow; then it looks as though we are navigating through a field of clover, upsetting the stems with the oars. She was completely at home here, maybe, for awhile, because there was no one else here; which means that there was no one but her and us; her and us, and these things and us. A few seagulls and sometimes a few swans that came to see us as well, puffing their feathers in anger when we came too close; other than that nothing and not a single living being (now that in the forest the birds had begun to quiet themselves);—so much so that there was nothing but the water and the lovely colors of the water, there was nothing but the sand, the stones. A ripple beside another ripple moving apart. We were with the boat, moving through the tip of an angle made from two folds, the sides of which grew softly wider like a piece of silk. She was still pulling a little on the left rope, we were heading straight for the buoy. Rouge and Décosterd let their oars drop and Décosterd ran forward just as we were going to hit the half-barrel painted in red and white (colors which can be seen the best and from afar) upon which the lantern was still lit but shed no light. She let go of the rudder. We saw Décosterd grab onto the lantern; he raised it up before him with its rounded glass and its pale little flame which gave only a little color in the pink air; then both men were pink across the entire front side of their person, from head to knees, on their mustaches, on their aprons. They handed the lantern to Juliette, she set it down beside her on the rear box. And then she was pink too, but on her side and on her shoulder, on her arm, on her left leg, while she sat there with her legs lifted off the floor to keep from bothering the work and she held her arm around her knees. For her, it was one of her cheeks, one of her legs, one of her bare feet. And all this time the men were pulling on the net; pink on their faces, they were tipped downward with both arms; they lean over, then straighten. They were bringing the net toward them. They pulled from the bottom to the top, it came up from the bottom to the top. They pulled on this trellis and up came this meshed espalier with the fruits it had gathered. First leaning over, then half-standing beside each other, all rosy in the light, they were working with their pink hands, going for the fruits of their labor that would then fall between their feet. Then, again, the color changed: it was when the sun finally came out from behind the mountain and they were repainted, relit, remade. So a flame twists upon their hands and between their fingers, then falls and extinguishes itself, but another is already coming, while all around you there are as many as you want, they are everywhere: at the crease of the smallest fold, upon the crest of the smallest wave.

Oh, she is exactly where she should be! When it came,

the sun didn't make the least distinction between her and the men. The sun loves her as much as us, some of its oldest friends, its daily companions. The sun hits against her cheek, upon her temple; the sun hits upon a part of her hair where she has flat tendrils that shine like steel blades. The texture of her skin is revealed on her neck, on the side of her neck and then forward, where her throat begins. She was in harmony with the light where everything round is smoothed. She held her arms around her legs. She turned herself backward toward the round rising sun above the mountain; it slipped off the mountain in little jumps as if the mountain was holding it back and the sun was saying, "Let me go!" Already the air was warming and already, because of this warmth, a strong odor of fish could be smelled all around you, at the same time these speckles of light shone on the side of her leg and there were splashes of light on her shoulder and along her body.

And so now Rouge, without dropping his net, said, "Well now, Miss Juliette, you're okay? You're not too bored?"

Already the net, fistful by fistful, had come to lean against the planking where it made a garland with its corks and weights; she laughs, she shakes her head.

She was with us, she was a kind of gilding put upon our life. Now our feet were covered up to our ankles with these tangled masses, like entrails freshly removed; a strong and sugary smell rose up. "We're almost finished," said Rouge, and then he looked at her again; so why did she lower her head just then? Just as they were reaching the second of the two buoys, then they hit the second half-barrel.

"Well, that's it," Rouge said. "Let's go, Miss Juliette, to work. We need you again…"

She shook herself, looking to the right and to the left. They turned back toward the shoreline. It was an ordinary fishing morning from five to seven or eight o'clock. Now the two men were rowing and had their backs to the earth; they were facing the sun. They were coming from the east and from the direction of Jerusalem, heading toward the west, and she watched the reeds at the mouth of the Bourdonnette grow larger and become a wall, and in front of this wall and out quite far into the lake was a yellow spot on the water. They were moving toward the high cliff, then they were turning a little, and from there they could see the house on the shore with its three-colored roof. No one was anywhere; it's not yet time for swimming; only vague noises could be heard from the village, beneath the silent vineyards. The girl was directing, the men were rowing.

They land.

It was just one of those fishing mornings; again Rouge looks at her. Décosterd had just left with the wheelbarrow; Rouge had gone to hang up the net. Contentedly, he watches her. He had filled his pipe, he was pulling on it, by sucking his cheeks in on the short wooden pipe. The smoke came off him through all sorts of little holes in his bushy mustache.

"Well," he said suddenly.

Everything was in order; we could see the well-stretched net was hanging with its transparent wall like a little fog rising straight up from the ground.

"Well! Things aren't so bad with this work, with your new profession, or what?" He pulls again on his pipe; another white puff rises up from his mustache. "It's just that it's a lovely line of work."

He indicates the net, the water, the sky, the house. "A lovely line of work for everyone, a good profession for you and for me, it's a man's work and it's a woman's work, a profession made up of two halves... Isn't that a coincidence!"

Because he was going back to the same old idea that had

surprised him: "It seems like we'd been waiting for you," is what he said, and then, "we were missing you, it's funny, and then you…"

He hesitated.

Then, "You…you were missing us, too, maybe, because here everything is calm and that's what we need, us, and that's what you needed… doesn't it just work out!"

He was saying these things, she was listening in silence; he raises his hand, "Calmness and freedom… just look at everyone else, land people I mean, because we're water people and it makes a big difference… everyone else… You saw what it was like, you had the chance to realize… These people at the café, Milliquet and everyone, eh? Attached to the soles of their shoes; yes, all these winemakers or the people who cut the hay and rake the hay, these owners of a corner of a pasture, of a part of a field, of a tiny piece of the land. You see all of them forced to follow a path and always the same one, between two walls, between two hedges, and here this is my home and next door it's not. It's full of rules over there, full of No Trespassing…they can't go left nor right… As for me… for us," he says, "we go where we want. We've got everything because we have nothing."

He'd begun a speech that had jumped from his lips despite himself, but now he couldn't stop and was making gestures to accompany the speech.

"Nothing stops us, we go where we want, we do what we want… See if you can find anyone, even at this hour, or anywhere, who could stop us from doing what we like and isn't that great? While they all live in smallness, with their 50 square meters, just enough to turn yourself around in…"

He says, "Miss Juliette?"

He interrupted himself suddenly, cutting off his lofty sayings.

"I think we're going to be able to make arrangements...we'll be able to arrange all this." Then he continued, "Here, you see, we go forward if we want and where we want; no neighbors, no walls, no edges, no barriers, no rules... So, tell me, would this suit you? If we made arrangements all the same..."

He doesn't finish the thought that particular day; and as for the girl, she listened, then nods her head two or three times as if saying yes. It was one of those fishing mornings.

That same afternoon, it came about that Rouge and Décosterd were busy working the nets; the girl, she was in her room. The men were outside and in the heat, next to the shed, between the net poles; she had gone to go sleep for a bit, at least we guessed she'd needed to sleep as people do in the middle of the day in those far away countries from which she came. Both men had their heads bent beneath their caps. There was a little noise like stones rolling. Rouge raises his head. It was Marguerite, little Marguerite from Milliquet's. She was standing up on top of the hill that edged the shoreline; she was up there among the bushes in a place you couldn't arrive from coming from the village without striking through the fields. And yet, it was really her, in her high-necked black dress with little white flowers; reddened cheeks, for the first time, from having run and hair more curly and wild than usual, and she was looking all about her with the abrupt movements of a bird.

"It's about Miss Juliette..."

She looks quickly all around her to make sure no one can see her, but the trees, the shrubs, even her position on the hillside all hide her from any view; so now she continues, speaking quietly.

"There was a terrible fight between Mr. Milliquet and his

wife...and so, I...I had something to buy in the village and so came quickly to tell you... Because," she says, "he's going to come... Yes, Mr. Milliquet," she says. "He said he was going to come get her himself. He said it was his right... He's going to come get Miss Juliette, and he said that if you don't let her go he would lodge a complaint... His wife is asking him for 20,000 francs... 20,000 francs, can you imagine that? I think some papers came, because he owes some money on the house. And his wife was yelling that he's ruined her. I think it was her money that he'd put on the house. She said to him, 'And my 20,000 francs, you scoundrel, where are my 20,000 francs?' He said, 'Your 20,000 francs, you want your 20,000 francs? Ok, you'll get them, I promise you, only you're going to let me... Now shut up! So well, you're ruined? Just wait...you know why you're ruined...' He said, 'No later than this afternoon...and we'll see about all this... Rouge will hear me out...there's the law; if necessary, I'll bring the police...' He's going to come, he's going to come, Mr. Rouge."

"He won't come," said Rouge.

"He will, because he even said to his wife, 'You're going to go up to your room and then you'll stay there, don't come down again...' Oh, he's coming, he'll surely come..."

"We'll see about that."

"And the girl, how is she?"

"She's just fine."

"That's good, but now I've got to get back. So, tell her, won't you? Be sure to tell her..."

"Not necessary. I'm the one going somewhere, to Milliquet's," said Rouge.

He wanted to say more, but little Marguerite had already run off, sliding from one tree to the next in the high grass of the orchard. Rouge stayed where he was a moment; he shook his head two or three times; then he raises an arm, calling to Décosterd.

He said to Décosterd, "All in all, it's better this way. This whole mess needs to be cleared up... I'm going over there right away. At least he'll know what he'll have coming to him if he ever comes bothering me... wait for me; I'll be back in a half hour..."

Then he seemed to hesitate, having turned halfway toward the house, and at first it was as if he were going to give in to this movement; but then, abruptly, he gave in to the opposite movement.

He brought his cap forward and strode off just as he was, wearing only his trousers and his shirt.

"And you..." he'd also said to Décosterd, "you stay put, keep an eye on what's happening."

Had she heard? Had she guessed at what had just happened? Or maybe it's just that a person gets bored?

She must have at least guessed that Rouge had just left, as he sometimes did in the afternoons; she must have also thought that Décosterd hardly mattered and then, because of where he was on the other side of the shed, it was possible for you to slip outside without being seen;—she'd gone to a corner and picked up her old dust-colored coat, the same she was wearing the day she'd arrived. She slips along the wall of the house; she is nothing but a gray spot on the gray rocks, she is nothing but a sand-colored spot on the sand. Now the house was between her and Décosterd, she hadn't been seen; next she reaches the reeds and the path through the reeds. Arrived at the bank of the Bourdonnette, she went to the left toward the fish warden's path; taking it up to the big road, you could make it to the village, and she must have known it, but not known the path very well. She went along the base of the bank, which climbed ever higher; which is why she had to raise her

head: she couldn't see anything on the village side, to her
left, because of the bank and the trees, and even more so
on her right where the steep cliff towered suddenly with its
coat of pine trees. She couldn't see anything and so she
picked up her pace even further, like she was worried and
impatient to be able to know where she was; then maybe
she realized that the path was going to be longer than she'd
thought. In this way, she entered the slimmest part of the
narrow pass where all around you is the forest and beneath
you the Bourdonnette is making a great sound of voices,
like being at Milliquet's when the café is full, with
discussions everywhere and fists slamming on the tables.
She didn't hear right away that someone was walking a little
above her in the bushes. He came out of the middle of all
the noise, like once before already, like on the terrace at
Milliquet's; he was suddenly right in front of her. She didn't
make the slightest noise; the Savoyard said nothing also, but
beneath his mustache he was laughing silently, baring his
teeth. He came toward her with his arms outstretched, she
jumps backwards. She saw right away that if she went back
on the path the way she had come, there was a big chance
she'd be cut off and her instinct brought her to put as
much distance as possible between herself and the man,
because he was coming from above down toward her; then
it's also maybe the youthful confidence one has in one's
blood, the strength of one's breath; so she races into the
forest, straight down the hill—hindered, but also defended
by the dense branches she has to first push through but
which also whip strongly backwards, and the man, the man
gets them full in his face. He was stopped for a second; this
short time was enough for her to then let herself fall to the
base of the hill; once down, she gets rid of her coat, she
can hear a burst of laughter. A hedge of alders making a
thick wall along the shore appeared, at the same time there
was a last slope; she throws herself into it, misses her mark,

but she had enough time to raise her hands into the branches and took a fistful, enough that she holds herself steady and hangs a moment, suspended, but her weight brought her downward, while the Savoyard is stopped again. She hears him swear, she goes forward, she falls into the water, she goes forward into the water, hiking up her skirt; she hears, amidst the sound she is making on the stones and which is added to the sound of the current, that he's called out to her, that he yelled something to her, but, looking backward at him over her shoulder, and now she is laughing, because she's seen that he just lost his cap and his hair has unrolled and is hanging over his eyes. She brings her shoulders up to her throat, then a deep breath, all full of laughter and air; she is like someone playing a game; all the while holding her arms out not to lose her balance. She laughs, she moves forward, and he, at the same time, throws himself toward her with an angry movement, but now already the entire width of the Bourdonnette separates them and he slides and goes to the side, his arms in the water up to his shoulders. She has already made it to the other bank; once on the shore, she immediately starts to climb. The terrain on this side is of a completely different nature. Beneath the pine trees were shelves of soft stones, nothing but steep terraces covered in a thick moss, separating everything; all of this rising up very high and at the top, facing south under a shadow where, above you, are openings, like wells of sunlight, pointed downward. These patches of sunlight made circles on the moss. She was in one of these sun circles for a moment; she climbed the hill using her hands and her feet. She climbed through the black earth, soil like coffee grounds with particles that enter your skin. Thick clods of moss came up between her fingers; she bit into this moss with her fingers like they were teeth. Oh, we can see again what kind of person she is while she climbs like this in her youth and her strength, going around one of these stone benches or even climbing it straightaway by gripping the roots that hang down from the crevices like beards or hair. Every once in a while, she turned around. We could see him, unable to follow her. He was outstripped. His hat was off, his hair a mess, out of breath; his red belt was undone, had started to drag behind him; which made him stop. She gets further ahead, she puts more and more ground between them. And now she makes it to the top of the ravine. Now before her was the forest floor, stretching forward with its tall tree trunks, each with enough space between them to run around freely. She could go left as clearly as right or straight, going back easily to the shore if she went right, getting quickly to the road and the houses if she went left. She would have had all the time she needed. But, suddenly, we see her stop, then she retraces her steps, she leans over the edge of the ravine, "Are you coming?" she says. "We're waiting for you…" She leans over the Savoyard. "What a coward! A coward! He doesn't dare!" because he hadn't yet started moving again, but the word reached him, so he throws himself forward.

"Oh, there you are!" she said.

She hadn't yet moved, and yet he was pulling himself up again: she hadn't moved, having leaned further forward to watch him more closely, but the top of the ravine is an overhang; there was an outcropping of soft earth that suddenly gives way beneath her; the nearly vertical incline receives her immediately and holds her straight by the two shoulders; she slides from the top to the bottom, she slides directly into the Savoyard in the moss and the black earth into which her heels make two lines; she sees him just beneath her and rising quickly toward her (or seeming to rise toward her), without having to make any movement;

she sees his teeth showing beneath his mustache, all he had to do was open his arms; only the shock was so strong that he falls as well, at the same time he grabs her and threads his arms around her body and holds on with all his might; he turns halfway around; her momentum makes him turn around and he is brought to the side of the hill where she is now hanging over the edge, leaning, then she's carried over, and he's carried over with her; they roll one over the other; this whole time he hasn't let her go, the whole time she feels his entire body against hers, feels his breath against her neck and the heat of his face against her own because he's brought his mouth forward; they roll, they roll several times; sometimes they're looking at the ground, sometimes the air, as the world turns upside down; there is a strong smell; it smells bitter, it smells damp, it smells like mold and rotting leaves; then she smells him, a more dangerous smell and coming closer because suddenly they've stopped rolling, they've just hit a tree trunk that holds them steady; he is on his knees, she is lying on her back, she sees his eyes coming closer, closer, getting larger, taking up all the space in front of her and coming to her; he still hasn't let her go, he still has his arms around her body; but we still haven't gotten to know her, or not completely; with a sudden movement, she makes his eyes leave her face, they ravish her face as she turns it, twisting her face and offering her neck which is raised up and her bodice opens from the top to the bottom; we can hear the sigh he lets out, but before the sigh can finish a kind of muffled yell takes its place, he brings his left hand to him; she is standing and he is standing, but he less quickly than her; he shakes his wrist twice because of the blood that is flowing along it; he ran, she is running in front, he grabs her by the sleeve and the sleeve gives way; so this is how we are treated! What does one expect, amidst these men?

Where is one to go? What is one to do? But her lovely shoulders shine in the sun now falling again on her, and she's again at the river; he has fallen behind: we see on his left hand the slim little crosshatches where he's bleeding, and this time his anger is the strongest, which makes him lose control of his movements; again she has time to turn right from where she is standing in the river bed, doubtless fearing she'll be stopped on the other side; she heads upstream, she is in the water up to her knees, but the slippery rocks on the river help her because he's wearing shoes with nailed soles and she has espadrilles, which is why she continues; again, she can turn her head, she sees him sliding with each step and blinded by splashes, falling sometimes onto his knees and onto his hands, her high clear laugh bursts out, which spurs him on, exciting him; the Bourdonnette widens further, opening up away from the ravine and into the beginning of the valley.

She is beautiful in the sunshine. He sees this beauty again.

But at the same time he's seen that this beauty will escape him, because Bolomey's little house has appeared with its low roof that touches the grassy hill behind into which the house is half-buried; and, out from Bolomey's little house, Bolomey has appeared.

He stands for an instant at the door, not understanding, then he goes back into his house.

She has left the riverbed; the Savoyard has also gotten out, trying to cross the hillside at an angle to cut her off.

Bolomey comes back out, his gun in his hands.

The other man sees the beauty of her shoulders shine one last time, and then, for an instant, the beauty shimmers in his own eyes; then there was nothing, even this he may no longer possess. It is escaping him. This beauty is escaping, it is extinguished.

There is nothing now but this little yellow-skinned man with his droopy mustache, a man walking forward slowly, continuing slowly two or three steps; then, because the Savoyard had still not stopped, we see him tilt the barrel of his rifle and slip the cartridges inside...

She is breathing deeply. She takes the air in so deep it reaches below her ribs; it rises back up, lifting her shoulders and making a great wrinkle in the skin of one shoulder and on the other side of her neck.

She let herself fall backward against the rise of the door. All is well. She breathes deeply. All is well and beautiful in the world. The sky is again above you in one piece, it is again immobile. She takes another deep breath, she breathes in the good air like something well-earned. She is going to be free,—she had forgotten that someone was there...

It's Bolomey, holding his shotgun under his arm. He said, "You'd better go in, Miss." He drops his eyes while speaking, and so she lowers her own. "We'll try to get you some clothing, although we're a bit short on women's clothing..."

He went in first.

And he's just gone into the second room, from there he called to Juliette, "Listen, I've found you a jacket, Miss. It's one of my hunting jackets. If you'd like to come in, there are some thread and needles on the dresser..."

The lovely countryside beneath the sky remained outside the door. It was an airless little room, in which, despite the fine weather, it is dark. He went out, he left her alone. Docilely, she did what he told her to do. She put on the gray-green cloth jacket with its large back pocket and its metal boars' head buttons. She looks at herself in the small black-spotted mirror. She sews up her skirt with its large rips hanging against her feet, revealing her knees...

Rouge had been back already for some time; his meeting with Milliquet had not lasted very long. He'd only been gone for a half-hour when Décosterd saw him coming back; he was walking with his head forward as if his head was too heavy, his cap pushed backward as if his head had swollen up. His face was even more flushed than usual and his mustache seemed lighter and whiter than before, while a thick vein beat in his temple and another fat vein stuck out from the side of his neck.

He came back, he said nothing.

He stops before Décosterd who is still working on the nets, still going along with the shuttle between the links; Décosterd looked at him with his one eye, an eye that saw as well as two eyes; he looked at him quickly, but said nothing. And Rouge said nothing. Décosterd asked him nothing, because he didn't need to ask him; we watch Décosterd take up his knife, cut the thread, close the blade of his knife.

Rouge makes a movement with his shoulders. A button on his cotton sweater comes undone.

At the opening of the Bourdonnette, just where the water has a yellow color, a colony of seagulls were lit up from this side and turned into a series of white dots (and they become black dots when they're lit from the other side).

Rouge suddenly said, "You haven't seen Juliette?"

We see that the house is extraordinarily still, nothing is moving on the shoreline, nor around the house, nor on the roof, nor at the windows: no smoke, no reflection in the glass, and Rouge says, "Juliette? You haven't seen her?"

"No."

"She didn't go out?"

"I don't know; I haven't moved."

Worry pushes Rouge forward. He walks over to the front of the house; he listens, standing on the front step. He listens, nothing can be heard.

He walked into the kitchen, he makes the bench scratch on purpose because maybe she's sleeping. Nothing.

He yells, "Juliette!" He raises his voice, "Juliette! Juliette!"

He sees the new door with its fresh paint and he stands in front of it for a moment, like it is going to open; it doesn't open, he pushes through...

Oh, how is it that one's heart is resigned so soon? He knew that no one would answer.

He goes out, he yells to Décosterd, "You didn't see if she took the boat?"

And Décosterd answers something, but Rouge is already inside the shed because it's easy to go and look himself: yet he knew already that the oars would be there.

The oars are there; he knew it. There was shade on the flat stones. The stones looked wet; the entire shoreline around him looks like it's been rained on; the reeds in the distance have gone gray, having lost their lovely white and green color. They are white at the base, green on top, but not for him once he's gone into them, having wanted to check the boat anyway, because one never knows with this girl: she might have left without the oars, which is what he tells himself on the path between the two walls of reeds; but at the same time he doesn't believe it, and, in fact, both boats are there. The *Juliette* is there, freshly painted, with its green exterior and its yellow interior; the boat is waiting calmly for someone to come, at the end of its chain, and no one has come, and no one is coming. Oh, there is no one and everything looks wet, dark, in the air; it's dark on the cliff where Rouge looks for a moment, and where there is no one between the thorny bushes, the little oak trees, the tufts of soapwort with their purple flowers and high stalks; no one higher up either on the moss-fringed border, in this trimming of moss we see hanging between two leaning tree trunks whose branches reach into the sky...

And it's much later, as he was heading back, but he didn't guess at first that it was her.

He saw Bolomey, he saw only that someone was with Bolomey.

Bolomey goes forward to meet Rouge; the girl, she waits further away in the jacket that is too big for her with its metal buttons with those visible boars' heads.

She was waiting, Rouge hadn't recognized her; then we see Bolomey approach him; so suddenly Rouge raises his head.

We hear him say to Bolomey, "How many of these shotguns do you have?"

He had looked at the ground for a long time, then quickly raised his head; he asks the question.

He starts again, "You'll have to lend me one. We might need it."

X

"Oh, Juliette, what were you thinking? You didn't want to stay with us? Is there maybe something in our way of life that doesn't suit you?"

He had sat her down in front of the house on the bench, it also freshly repainted with the same color they had used on the shed.

It was that same evening, after sunset, but it was still pink on the wet stones along the shoreline and on the dry stones, too: it was pink along the shore with two different pinks.

"You're in no danger here, I promise you that here you'll be well protected..."

He went into the kitchen, he came back with the rifle that Bolomey had lent him.

She looks at the rifle without saying a word; so he sets it on the ground, the butt to the ground against the wall.

"But if it's you that wanted to leave..."

Then he continues, "It's ready to be used, it's loaded with shells; that isn't too much for these savages..."

And then coming back to his first idea, "We would have really liked you to be happy; we would have really liked it... Tell me, Miss Juliette, Juliette....yes, Décosterd and me, both of us. Didn't we do what we could? Tell me, are you in need of anything?"

She shook her head; very slowly and twice, she shook her head.

"So?"

He stopped in front of her. He went out for a moment into the pink light, then came back and stood before her; he leaned toward her a little: "So?"

He changes his tone: "When everything was falling into place so well, you know. Everything was getting settled so easily, despite Milliquet; but I'll deal with him…"

She shakes her head again.

"You know they're all spying on you, there are two or three of them spying on you."

"Well!" he says, "That's what men are about! Not worth much − meanness, jealousy, envy. And plenty of greed… this Savoyard…"

Now he was throwing his sentences out haphazardly, he wasn't finishing them.

"You must know that he won't let you go so easily… they're watching in the woods…they can see everything from up there…"

He motioned through the pink light toward the overhang of the cliff; he had to raise his arm: "From up there… if they feel like it, huh! From up there… And still, this Savoyard, if we wanted to, it wouldn't be difficult to get rid of him, we could lodge a complaint…"

She shakes her head for the third time.

"Oh, I know!" he says without understanding, "we won't lodge a complaint. But for everything else…it's just that you don't know it yet: Milliquet wants to take you back… everyone is against us."

He thought she would be surprised; she didn't seem surprised, at least as much as we can see in the remaining light in which a gray cinder has come to place itself over the lovely pink coals that have now gone out, the cinder hides the coals and all is dark around us. We see Juliette simply raise her head, look at him, and say nothing.

"Yes," Rouge said, "It's like that... And, Milliquet, it's only because he's jealous, but his jealousy has got hold of him. And he won't dare come here now that he knows what would be waiting for him..." He shows the rifle. "He knows very well that we have all that we need to welcome him, but this business isn't yet resolved. And the Savoyard, that's just one problem. And Milliquet, that makes another, that makes two... But that's not all. Because there are still others..."

He makes a circle with his arm, including the entire shoreline in front of him: "All these boys, as far as I know... all those that want to, who would like to, big Alexis, little Busset, even that old drunk Chauvy..."

He was growing angry.

"Yes, the whole lot of them, as far as I know, and where does it come from? But they are everywhere and they're spying on you. And so, if you say that you're fine here..."

She makes a sign that means yes.

"So you say you've got nothing to complain about here... from us. Not from Décosterd and not from me..."

She makes a sign that means no.

"So why did you run off? Juliette, my little Juliette. And why did you want to leave me... leave us?"

But she shakes her head again; she interrupts him. She said something to him.

He listens to her speaking, speaking with her funny hoarse accent: he listens to her, he shouts out, "Oh, my God, you had to say! So, it's because of the little hunchback? It was him you were going to look for?"

She is talking now, talking a lot. She gets mixed up in her sentences, she laughs; she confuses them, she straightens them out; she can't find the words; she invents them; she laughs again, and then he says,

"Why didn't you say anything to me?"

He laughs, too.

"But, listen, why didn't you say something? I would have gone and gotten him for you. He's alright with me; he doesn't count, he isn't dangerous... I understand...the little hunchback, my goodness! It's the music, I understand...Oh, Juliette, you really frightened me... I'm old, I was thinking you'd had enough of me. So it's the Italian... he's Italian, right? It's this Italian you want? Yes, the hunchback, the one who works for Rossi. I understand fine, it's his music. So, nothing easier than that...."

She was speaking, he was speaking:

"I'll go and get him for you tomorrow... I will get him as often as you'd like. We'll invite him to come whenever he likes. It's true he doesn't know anyone either, the poor boy, and anyway he isn't handsome, that doesn't bring people to him... But you're missing his music? Oh, I understand that! I'm like you, I miss it, too. You see, Juliette, we are so much alike..."

He stops suddenly.

"When will you turn twenty?"

"Next year, in March."

He counts on his fingers, "That's in eight months, a little more than eight months..."

He had started to walk again up and down. "The problem is that while we wait, he'll have the law on his side... Milliquet. But then you just get to choose. And if you're thinking the same way, we could... I need to get some more information. Juliette, I'm sixty-two years old, I could be your grandfather. But we could remove the first half of the word, if you like, because there's also a law for situations like this..."

She didn't speak.

He was walking with his hands in his pockets, up and down, in front of the water, where a star had appeared and was slowly rising, then coming down, like when we've thrown out the fishing line and the cork stays up to float.

And he changed his voice again to say, "While we're waiting, I forbid you to go far from the house. You understand, Juliette, I forbid you to go out alone."

Was he able to see how suddenly she lets herself fall forward with the top of her body and the weight of her head? How could he not see it?

She had placed her hands together: she slides them between her knees.

"As for the hunchback," Rouge started again, "It's agreed; tomorrow, I'll go get him for you."

They were spraying copper sulfate for the third or the fourth time because there are these new methods. We repeat the treatment nowadays up to six or seven times; as soon as a rain shower hits, they were running back up to their tanks. Up means behind the village, once you've passed the fields and the orchards, then the road, then more fields; up where the rise to the mountain begins with its walls. There had been several big summer rain storms; at once the men had started working the sprayer again;—all these men in their blue coveralls, moving up and down, up and down, between the vines; in their coveralls, their trousers, their shirts, their shoes, their blue straw hats, and with their blue faces, blue hands, ears, napes and neck, and blue mustaches;—the girl, she went up toward them with her basket. She was going up to bring the ten o'clock to her father and her two brothers. This is little Emilie. She was wearing a pretty cloth dress, striped, she was wearing a straw hat with a silk ribbon, she had such lovely blonde

hair: oh, what does one look for in life? She asks the trees
if they have seen him. She goes beneath the cherry trees
along a grassy path that is marked only by two ruts; My
God, how lonely she is! She raises her eyes, she sees there is
nothing, there is no one anywhere. No one but her little
shadow just to her left and just in front of her in the grass.
So she looks behind her where we can see the village falling
away, seen from above, with its roofs; but they don't count,
these roofs. Nor do the apple trees, nor the walnut trees,
nor the pear trees, nor all these fence posts, nor the line of
the railway, nor the train station; and, as we walk up higher,
we see the water growing wider and wider, and behind her
the mountains, hovering in the hot air like balloons ready
to take off. It's set down beside you for a short moment,
and we are set down next to it, for a short moment, and
then that's all. She continues on alone, with her shadow.
She sees the vineyards where the three men should be
waiting for her. The vineyards are behind a wall; we go in
through an opening drilled through the wall and closed
with a red-painted iron door; she sees the large lacy leaves
whose lovely green is spotted as if it has rained a blue rain.
And it has rained blue onto the ground, it has rained blue
onto the stones, onto the vine stakes, what does that matter
to us? She sees her father coming and her two brothers
beneath their copper sprayer tanks and their great rush
hats; they have mustaches like pieces of a wall that haven't
yet dried, they have chests like masonry work, they have
trousers like cement tubes. They said, "So there you are,"
they went to wash their hands. There is nothing. She rests
her basket against the wall, she pulls back the white linen
cover, she pulls out two bottles and puts them in the
shadow, prepares the knives, the glass, then she waits for
them to come back, because they eat without plates, just a
quick bite. And it's my father. And they come back. They

went to wash their hands, they come back: it's my father and my brothers, but they say nothing, because they have nothing to say; they haven't said anything to her, and this is also because they are hungry. They've sat down beside one another on the wall but a certain distance apart. The three of them are there, along the wall. We see the lake between their heads. There is a big space between their heads for all the things which come, and the air is bothered with a fly and a white or yellow butterfly, or maybe it's even a sail. What are we looking for? Because the men are here, but they're eating because they are hungry. They use their knives to cut the bread, then cut their cheese. They bring the piece of cheese to their mouths with the blade and then their hands go back down, while their jaws are moving. Their jaws go up and down; the men themselves do not move, do not speak. Their heads are hung forward, their arms are hanging and their legs hanging. It's as if they don't exist. Oh, what is wrong? What is wrong? And what happens then when you can't find anything anywhere to hold onto? When she sees the water between their shoulders, and that's all: we see the water around their heads, and that's all. Such distance! They are there, I am here, they are eating their bread and their cheese. She sees the water: such distance; she sees the air, she sees the trees: such distance, such distance! And over there, suddenly, in the bit of the wide fold made by the Bourdonnette beneath the cliff and the pine trees, a piece of shoreline appears; and surely he is there and he is there and I'm not there; Maurice is over there and I'm here, oh such distance! And of another kind. She lowers her head, she can't look anymore, she no longer has the strength; the men have seen nothing. They don't understand, these men who are my father and my brothers, because we cannot understand each other, because we are just set down next to one another, because we cannot communicate, because we are one, then one, then one; because there are them, there is him, there is me. And we all thought that he and I… I had everything because I had him… Everything slips away and she managed to hold back a sob, but the men are still eating and still drinking; they've noticed nothing, they've neither seen nor heard a thing. They pass the glass to each other, they smack their lips. They take their mustaches into their lips to wipe them off, they get up. And me, where am I supposed to go?

They pick up their copper spraying tanks, then go down to the cistern where they dip with the dipping ladle; she puts the bottles, the knives and the glass into the basket, where to go? And what are we looking for, what are we looking for?

She passes beneath the cherry trees again. Now her shadow is behind her and to the right. That is the only difference, nothing has changed; your shadow turns around you until you're dead and that's it.

She went into the village. People greet her, she answers; that's all. We know nothing about nothing, nor about anyone, nor about oneself. And then suddenly she stops. Suddenly, the thing she sees is Rouge walking in front of her, then he is taken away into the little street: and there was enough curiosity left in her heart to make her follow him.

She saw him enter behind the sheds, there where the workshop of the little Italian cobbler could be found.

This was while they were working in the vineyards, which meant that Rouge hadn't run into anyone or nearly anyone. No one but a few children on the shoreline, and one or two women in front of Perrin's at the water, but they had their backs to him and were doing the laundry. He hadn't seen

Emilie. He went behind the sheds until he arrived at the cement-framed door above which was a sign reading: *Cobbler*, in black letters on a white background. The cobbler was an old Italian man and Rouge knew him, because he could be met often walking through the village with his white mustache and his long Roman-style cape with one of the panels thrown over his shoulder, lying in folds around his neck. His name was Rossi, and Rouge knew him well; only he'd been taken to the hospital two months earlier for a double fracture of the leg. The hunchback was just his assistant. He'd only arrived, actually, a short time before Rossi's accident and so Rouge didn't know anything about him and no one knew anything about him. He'd appeared one fine day at Milliquet's with his accordion; we'd said, "He plays wonderfully well"; he'd come back and we'd said, "There aren't many like him." And after that, there was the scene with the Savoyard, and we hadn't seen him again. Where did he come from? We didn't know. And today Rouge is knocking on his door, but all he knew was that the other man was there, having seen him when passing by the window. We could still hear the sound of the hammer on the leather, then the sound stopped while someone yelled, "Come in!"

The other man was seated on a low stool, he couldn't have been seated on a chair with a back, and his head was leaning forward and he couldn't have held it straight or bring it backward. We see him turn his head toward you, with his lovely eyes that shone, then are extinguished; he raises his rounded hammer again over the brass nails. And Rouge moves forward a little, Rouge gets comfortable; he put his hands in his pockets, he says, "I haven't come for shoes; those of us in my profession, well, we don't wear them out so much. We wear out the skin on our feet, our own leather…"

He begins with jokes about the work bench and the tools that cover it: pieces of leather, pins, little pots of pine-pitch glue, cobbler knives, awls; he says something about every item he looks at: and then, "And so it isn't the cobbler that I'm looking for, Mr...."

He searches for the name, he realizes he doesn't know it.

"Because everyone agrees about it, I'm the first one to say so, that there aren't two like you...And maybe you don't know..."

He looks at the hunchback, who looked at him as well, but it was hard for him since Rouge had stayed standing.

"It's after this mess with the Savoyard. Oh! you know, we were all sorry about it. But we're hoping... I wasn't there that night, but she... You must remember Juliette, Miss Juliette..."

The hunchback said nothing, and then now he gets up. It's hard for him to get up because of the weight of his back pushing him forward.

He got up, he said nothing; he goes to the second door that opens to the next room, he disappears a moment, he comes back.

And then Rouge says, "Ah!...Oh, good, I see that it didn't get too banged up, your instrument, but it's also that you're so good with it... It was hard to find leather, was it? And glue, if it can be glued...Oh, it works wonderfully well after all...Oh, it's just as good as it was before, congratulations... Yes, she's going to be so happy..."

Then he stopped because he couldn't make himself be heard anymore.

"I haven't told you everything yet, Mr. ..."

He is obliged to stop speaking...

"She's the one who sent me..."

The other man makes his fingers run quickly up and down the mother-of-pearl keys, then he presses both hands on the bellows for a chord.

"She's been missing... yes, that, your music. She asks if you'd like to come. She misses it. In her country..."

He starts again, "Really though, it isn't her country, her real country is this country; her name is Milliquet like her uncle and there isn't a name more from here than that name... but okay she was born over there and was raised over there, and so over there they're always playing music and dancing... And over there, according to what she says, they play a lot of guitar, but she says that there are a lot of people from your country working on the railroads in the mountains and they play the same instrument as you... It's easy to sympathize with her...she hasn't settled in yet..."

He was interrupted again. The music started again.

All these high little notes, then the low notes; and it was like disturbing a bee hive to steal the honey. Rouge was taken up inside it. It flew at him from all around, against and into his face. He could no longer hear what he was saying. He has to wait a moment. Then he can hear himself saying:

"It's just like the sails; did you know she makes fun of ours because they're made from cloth? Over there, they have woven sails, they're made like pleated mats; they have raffia mats and they're square. She makes fun of ours because they're pointed and they're white... it's called Santiago over there. But it's all worked out wonderfully well in the end, because there's water over there too; so she knows how to row, she knows how to fish, she knows how to swim; and so I told myself that she would find all that here too; except for the music..."

A single little note held long, and then two or three more

trotting above it like a mouse stepping across a ceiling, and then:

"But if you'd like to come... Because she...because I'm inviting you and it's me giving the invitation of course. We'll have a drink together... it would make her happy..."

The little notes continue on.

"You, you're not the same... the same as the others. All the other men, these ruffians... the Savoyard, these boys...you, no, it isn't the same thing," Rouge says, while the little unwinding notes seemed to unroll themselves in time with the words he was saying, "I trust you... and I even want you to be careful, in case someone sees you coming to my house. It would be better if Décosterd came to pick you up... Do you want to come this evening? We'll surprise Juliette. I told her that I would come to get you, but she doesn't know yet that I've come... you would play a little tune for her at the house, a surprise..."

He was happy, he began to laugh:

"You'd like to, so it's agreed... tonight. I'll send Décosterd to get you."

The other man raises his eyes once again, with difficulty, toward Rouge, his eyes shone and then went out; he gave only a nod and again the air exploded between the ceiling and the floorboards, and then fell in a thousand little fragments around you, like glass, like standing in a greenhouse and all the squares of glass fall to the ground;—in front of the work bench; in front of the little pots, the awls, the rounded hammers, the cobbler knives, the pieces of leather.

A nod of the head, to say yes, after which Rouge backed up a little; and the lovely bellows presses together, stretches apart, twists, untwists, finally folds into itself with little creases along one side, and is smooth and rounded on the other.

"Thanks very much," Rouge was saying. "Until tonight, then... no, don't get up."

He didn't get up. Rouge opens the door. Now the music was coming from the other side of the wall and from behind the windows; but it kept coming. He leaves, the music was following him. It followed him into the small street; only there did it come apart, unravel and wear down bit by bit in the air, fall into pieces behind him. All this time he is walking quickly beneath the sunshine; and it's lovely out, these twigs of straw shining like golden watch chains in the dust. It's lovely out, these shadows thrown by the edges of the roofs and they are only along the edges of the path; all is carefully drawn with a ruler. Nevertheless, at the corner he stepped into the one thrown by Milliquet's terrace with its plane trees that finally have all their leaves, but it's the least well drawn of all of them and it takes up too much space. And also, we don't want to show Milliquet that we've put ourselves out for him. We'll show him that we're not afraid. Rouge cuts across the corner of the terrace. He passes just next to the iron gate and we can see the green tables between the bars, then we see Milliquet; and we see that this is a café whose sole customer today is its owner; if he fancies, he can always serve himself!

"Hi there," Rouge yells, "are you on holiday?"

And then we hear the other man call him back, but Rouge walks on, happy to raise his arm as if to say, "another time," which really means, "Today, I've got better things to do."

Today, we have better things to do.

"Rouge, listen, I've got something to tell..."

"Sure, mate ..."

"Something important to tell..."

"Okay, another time, mate ..."

"Do you hear that, ladies?" he said to the women with their washing as he passed by.

They are on their knees leaning into their washtubs, they turned their heads. "You heard that, ladies, he's asking for me, but have a great day, ladies..."

"And then," he also said, "it's too beautiful today to waste any of it..."

"See you later, ladies."

They rub against the washboard with a square piece of Marseille soap that is too big for their hands, but they end up wearing down the corners and it gets smaller; they froth up white suds; out on the blue water with the swans, we see these other white spots bobbing. Rouge walks on.

And now he's at home but he didn't find her because she was in her room, but so much the better. At noon when she finally came out to eat, she said nothing, but so much the better. She doesn't speak, so much the better. It was like she was elsewhere again, so much the better; she seems sad, so much the better...

Now we know why, he is thinking, and we'll surprise her.

And a little later, he said to Décosterd, "Listen, Décosterd, go to the Railway Café and ask them for two bottles of Aigle†... No, get six...go ahead and get a half dozen. There's room in the bag. Get a half dozen bottles of Aigle 23, because it's good stuff. You remember we drank a bottle with Perrin last year, when Perrin lost his bet... and then listen, Décosterd, once you've got the bottles, take the back roads... you know where Rossi's workshop is? Good! Just go in there, the little hunchback will be there; he's going to come play some music for us... I told him you would come get him, because it's better he doesn't come alone... bring him with the bottles and don't be bothered about passing in front of Milliquet's once it's

† *Wine from the village of Aigle*

130

on your way… and try to arrange things to let one of the bottle necks show; that'll make him even angrier. A person shouldn't hold back if we're of the mind to throw a party…"

"You understand," he says. "She was getting bored; it's natural, we were living like old men here…"

"Hey," he says, "we're not so old as all that, we're not actually old men, finished old men, old and washed up… are we, Décosterd?"

This was while they were finishing to hang up the nets as the sun set, behind the shed; Décosterd went to wash his hands with soap.

He goes to the edge of the shore and leans over in the place where the stones give way to a narrow margin of sand, onto which the little waves always play, climbing up and falling back, like little girls on a hillside.

A wave comes. Décosterd takes it in his hands.

The soap doesn't foam easily, and not right away because the water in the lake is very soft water: it doesn't have a bite.

It takes a while to make suds, it takes time before we can cover our hands with white gloves.

So Décosterd was able to let a few waves come and go; then comes one he takes up again in his hands to rinse them.

He went to get the bag; Rouge gave him a bill to pay for the wine.

So then Rouge waits. He goes to and fro to the door. He went and then came back a minute. Suddenly, he must have thought of something. He goes back inside the house, like he was in a hurry; but he *was* in a hurry. What he had to do, actually, was go hunting for his suit at the back of his closet, it had been a long time since he'd worn it; a blue lambswool suit. Luckily, there was no need to light the gas lamp, and he could see well enough to knot his tie, his fat fingers rushing against the underside of the stiff fabric and amidst the confusion of these silk lacings, standing in front of the little aluminum framed mirror hung from a hook on the window, in the messiness of your belongings, in the dust, in the dirt, because his room had remained as it was and we hadn't worked on it during the renovations.

All that mattered for the moment was that he was ready in time. He was ready in time. He was even early enough to go and meet those who were coming when they came. It was starting to get dark because the sky was covered with clouds; we could just see the height difference between the two men. We could also just see the instrument in its waxed cloth case making a hump, another hump on the hunchback's hip. Rouge waves to tell the two men to wait. We were just starting to see a little pale white star in a strip of green sky, between two clouds, to the west. "Oh good," Rouge says as he walks up, "I can see we can count on you…" And to the hunchback, "You're just fine, you, you're a real… Thank you. Only, I wanted to tell you… hey, Décosterd, you've got the wine?"

And as Décosterd had the wine, all was fine. "Listen," Rouge says to Décosterd, "Hold onto the bottles for a minute. We don't want her to hear us walk. We'll keep back, the two of us, by the nets… and you (he was no longer talking to Décosterd), you go quietly up to the house, you go and sit down on the bench. Don't start playing until you're ready, but then give it your all…"

We did as Rouge said. She must not have heard the hunchback as he went along so carefully; as for us, she couldn't hear us. We see the hunchback who goes to sit near the bright square of light that the lamp made through the open door onto the stones. He was half-shadowed, half-lit. He is a little bit of night in the half-night. We see him, ever so carefully and already seated, bring the accordion up and set it crossways on his knees. He was like a mother undressing her child, so careful was he with his fingers along the buttons of the case. And he doesn't start right away, because we see him first raise his head like he was thinking; and after a moment he raced his fingers across the keys into the empty air...

It goes without saying: he had a bit of genius. (Décosterd was something of a connoisseur.) These high notes, these low notes, the melody, the chord, all of this jumped at once like a shot from a cannon. And then he had rhythm, something you don't see every day. And him, well, just look at him! Little nothing arms, skeletal hands, a body... a body, you well know, a body best not mentioned; none of this stopped him from having the power to make the world dance. He would bring the waves over to you from the other side of the lake, I tell you, and they wouldn't come when they wanted or how they wanted, but only when and how he wanted. He began with a little bit of introduction in triple time and a little dance tune; but Rouge had told him to try to play something she might know, a tune from over there, from her country; so now he is playing a song. And then...

Neither Décosterd nor Rouge had moved. They saw everything from where they were standing. First we saw this shadow come inside the frame of the window, and it moved across the white curtains; it grew larger, became smaller. There, too, was some preparation, because two hands were now raised, moving to the face and into the hair; then everything deformed and the whole shadow lost its shape, lengthening and slimming, while both men remained where they were. The accordion was now playing with scales, runs of clear little notes slipping through one's fingers like polishing a necklace and letting it hang in the air to highlight its beauty. Rouge and Décosterd had not moved from their spot; the girl had not yet appeared, but we were waiting for her. This is when Rouge said, "And the bottles?" They were still on Décosterd's back. Décosterd hadn't even thought to take off his bag. "My God!" Rouge said. "We've got to put them quickly to chill." He takes the bag Décosterd holds out, he goes down to the water, he comes back: "And you, go get the glasses. Hurry!" And he leans down, laying the bottles into the sand. And there was nothing but the gentle little waves that come with a soft quiet night like tonight; Rouge leaned over and squatted then, laying the bottles one beside the other. Décosterd had just gone into the kitchen. The hunchback on the bench hadn't even raised his head, quite the opposite, we see him put his head down and press his cheek against the flat of the instrument,—and the music swings again for a moment, then there is a break, then the swing starts again on a shorter, stronger rhythm; and Décosterd was just taking the glasses from the cupboard...

She was so light that we hadn't heard her open her door, we hadn't heard her come out. Her feet seemed to touch the ground without any weight. There was only the rustle of her skirt like when a lovely butterfly whispers against you with its wing, nothing but this rustle of fabric making Décosterd turn around; so he doesn't move, his glass in his hand. At this same moment, Rouge stands up; his arms hang down along his body, while the light coming through the open door is upon him, on his lovely navy blue wool suit, his white collared shirt, his tie, his fat mustache.

It's that she was more brilliant than ever before, it's that we hardly recognized her anymore.

Someone had to... but how to say it? Someone had to go to her where she was standing up by the door; and, before that, there were several things: up where she is standing, there is only one. Before, things came one by one to you, they were separate from each other, we could only hold onto to one thing at a time,—now, all these things are together and it's like they are one. But how to make oneself understood, and is this what needs to be said? Is this what they're all thinking in their heads, behind the bill of their caps, beneath their skulls? Alas! Fused forever, beneath Décosterd's close-cut hair and Rouge's nearly white and sparse head? We saw they hadn't made the slightest movement, not one nor the other. Décosterd still had his glass in his hand. We see Rouge standing with his hanging arms, and behind him, vaguely, the black spots of the bottles on the gray sand...

The lovely leather bellows suddenly stops pressing the folds together between the skinny little wrists which press it and hold it; she, her skirt turns once or twice more around her legs, then she throws off the weight of her hair, her head tipped all the way back.

Nothing moves anymore: we heard the silence come forth like the end of the world on its way. The end of our movement was like the end of all life. Nothing else happened, a great emptiness opened up and we fell inside it; we are still falling in it, we fall for a long time; then we had to come back to the other life, our former life.

Rouge was thinking he would clap, he didn't clap.

He stepped forward a little, he walks forward clumsily, and then he says, "So, now you see," he says, "Now, you see it's all right." The girl, she didn't know what to do; the girl, she was already no longer herself; she was out of breath, breathing hard, with difficulty; Décosterd places the glass he was holding in his hand onto the table.

He makes a light noise as he sets it on the table, and so Rouge, as if waking up, says, "Décosterd, pull the table to the side, that'll make some room... Give me a hand. We'll push it against the door to my room..."

The two men pulled the table to the side.

Then Rouge, "And now, the bottles, quick!" and he comes back with a bottle under each arm.

It's the other life that begins; we don't have the same freedom here.

He uncorks the bottles. He doesn't dare look at her. She was leaning up against the wall, she was waiting. She is still smiling with her shiny teeth. He doesn't dare look at those teeth. He keeps himself busy, he makes signs, he uncorks the two bottles, he says to Décosterd, "You've got all four glasses? It's just we don't have a lot of glasses..." Then he yells, "Hey, Mr. Urbain, won't you join in? We're waiting for you... won't you come drink with us?"

He filled the glasses with this gold, gold that is a little green, but lovely and limpid: at least we have this in our poor little life.

He raises his glass, full to the brim.

"To your health, Miss Juliette. Health and prosperity."

She raised her arm as well; he turns his eyes away.

Nonetheless it's a lovely little wine, it's cool, it's clear, it's fresh with taste, it's warm, they are speaking; but he doesn't dare speak anymore, he doesn't dare speak further, having now drunk to the health of the hunchback who came in.

Décosterd was watching between two swallows of wine that made his thin neck tip back, moldy with whiskers, on which his Adam's apple was like a sharp stone;—between two swallows, he was watching this handsome wool vest, the white shirt, the silk tie...

Only, that same night, she was awakened by the sound of the front door opening; she hears someone walking with muffled steps across the stones.

As a precaution, she didn't light the lamp in the beautiful new room where she is, but there was a little moonshine that came across to her bed. There was a very pale moon floating between two strips of clouds, like between the two sides of a strait where snow has fallen. Because of the moon it was light enough for her to see the front of the house clearly. All she had to do was push back the curtain. It was Rouge; he was barefoot, hatless. He'd only taken enough time to put a pair of trousers over his mostly open shirt. He was holding the rifle he'd borrowed from Bolomey. Surely, he'd heard some noise; the moon shone along the length of the polished steel gun barrels.

He went first toward the village, he comes back, he passes in front of the window; then he must have gone farther away toward the reeds and the cliff because she no longer hears anything.

XI

Maurice let himself drop onto the roof of the chicken coop; lowering himself over it then with both hands, he had only to let himself drop to the ground. Well before ten o'clock, everyone was sleeping in the big pink house where the master and mistress are lying in the old walnut bed that is big enough for two, where the maids are in their pine or iron beds, and the workers hired by the week sleep in the hay. He attached his shoes around his neck by their laces. His room looked out to the back of the house. The crossbars on the window could have cracked and no one would have heard him. He threw one leg over the supporting wall, then the other leg. He fell beside the trellis that was stretched between two reinforced concrete pillars, because Mayor Busset liked durability. They had replaced the wooden troughs with iron troughs. They'd had an electric motor installed in the barn. They'd purchased a mechanical bottling machine. They keep abreast of all forms of progress...

This was at the same time that Décosterd had begun feeling uneasy about Rouge; and little Maurice Busset was slipping outside his house through the window: Rouge had just taken Décosterd aside to tell him that people were prowling the shoreline at night. And Décosterd had just shrugged his shoulders; but now, just a little while later, he couldn't stop himself from thinking that Rouge maybe wasn't as wrong as he seemed. Décosterd was with the hunchback (and it was the third or fourth time he was bringing him back to his door), when he, too, seemed to hear someone walking beneath the trees.

Décosterd and the hunchback were following the edge of the water and had just reached the pine tree forest; this is where he thinks he hears footsteps and that someone was following them. He didn't say anything; the hunchback didn't seem to have noticed anything. It was a very dark night. Décosterd didn't even stop. Even if he'd had the feeling that someone was still following them; but he couldn't see a thing, the lights in the sky remained hidden behind their thick wrapping paper.

It was just a bit later, when Décosterd was alone: he heard someone approaching. This time, the steps were more distinct and were going up the same street that he was going down. Then the footsteps stopped; he understood someone was waiting for him.

"Oh, it's you, Mr. Maurice."

It's our mayor's son, a boy who's been well-raised. We couldn't see him, we saw only the white color of his straw hat.

He was rather pale and thin because he had studied. His father, the mayor, had made him finish his schooling. Each night he stepped over the window sill, he let himself fall down onto the roof of the chicken coop...

Even though the little street was empty, a long-standing caution had directed Décosterd; he took Maurice by the arm and pulled him behind the sheds. Here, nothing but hay, straw, farming equipment, tools, and nothing else, no living beings, only mice and cats, when this last lot want to do their job and aren't overly tempted by their rendezvous beneath the full moon in the orchards. No ears here, at least not the ones that can understand, and no eyes that can recognize you, which is something other than just seeing. Which is why he pulls Maurice behind the wall; then, following a question from Maurice:

"Oh, Mr. Maurice, you couldn't imagine… he's becoming crazy…he's got a rifle, you know… he borrowed it off of Bolomey… if you come, he's liable to shoot at you… it's gotten worse over the last few days…oh, the hunchback, yes, it's true, but Rouge says that the hunchback doesn't count, I think on account of his hump. And me, you say, but me, I've only got one eye… you see… you, you've got two eyes and no hump."

We heard Maurice's voice: "So, what've we got to do?"

"Drat it, I just don't know," said Décosterd.

We hear Maurice's voice: "It's just that it's for her; we're not going to be able to leave her there much longer. They don't know who she is, they don't see the difference… Yes (he hesitates, he lowers his voice), yes, you, maybe, which is why I came. I was thinking we might be able to understand one another. I come in the evening to listen to the music, and she, she comes out sometimes, and I can see you, you understand. Music and her, they go so well together, and you, you understand, but those others they can't understand and my father can't understand either. As the mayor, he's going to have to sort this mess out; and just this evening he was talking about it at supper; he said that if Milliquet lodges a complaint, we'll have to open an inquiry. And he also said, while he was talking, that there are institutions for these kinds of girls: so they'll send the police to get her…."

"That would be a bad thing," Décosterd said.

"That's why… what should we do? Okay, I'll tell you. I had an idea. Couldn't we get her to leave, if you were willing to help us? There are enough of us to do the job. There's Alexis, he wants to help. Alexis, Bolomey, you maybe… I have an old aunt in Bougy who lives alone; I could ask her to take the girl in. You, you would help us… In three weeks is the Fleur-de-Lys party… if she could come. Oh, it would be lovely if she could come. And it would be a good time..."

"And the hunchback?" asks Décosterd.

"He would come with her, he would accompany her. And then he could always go and see her later in Bougy, it isn't so far. So I'll tell my aunt to offer to take her in; she's the sister of my father's father; she loves me, she does whatever I want... we could surely arrange the thing; if only you'd give us a hand, because we can't do a thing without you, and you're the one who can help..."

There was a little silence. There was just enough time for Décosterd to bring his hand to the back of his neck and into his shaved hair beneath his cap; after which, we heard: "Well... it's Rouge I'm afraid of... and also, I think that it would be... yes, it would be too bad..."

And then another silence:

"We'll see about it."

Again another silence.

"Only, you've got to let me do it, okay? When is this party? ...Oh, it's the third Sunday in August...so it would be, wait, on the 15th... only the police better not come before, but they won't come before then. These kinds of inquiries always take forever. What will be hard is to make sure Rouge keeps calm until then, because he's deeply serious about it. But okay, I can help, Bolomey too... and you, on your side... and then there's the hunchback... we'll do our best, Mr. Maurice."

The rest of the words said by the two men get lost in the base of this windowless wall made of cement bricks, above which there is only the thick brown-black paper wrapping of the sky, all wrinkled up; while over there, in the café, we heard Milliquet's voice, to which laughter replied, and again we hear Milliquet's voice, but we laughed even harder;

nevertheless, we were entering a difficult period, an agitated period; the kind in which Décosterd hardly slept that night, after he returned to the little room he rented in the village; and, having thrown himself fully-dressed onto his bed, he lies there thinking...

The weather was bad for four or five days, we didn't go fishing; and then the fine weather came back, but we didn't go back to the fishing.

Sometimes Rouge went as far as the boats; other times he walked up the Bourdonnette along the fish warden's path; he never stayed away for very long.

It must be said, however, that he didn't notice anything to worry about anywhere, and that these shorelines had even become especially empty for the last two or three weeks.

The reason for this was that the great labors of the countryside were at their height;—and, the rest of us, we keep ourselves focused on the water, but there are only a few of us. Most everyone else, those that belong to the land and keep their backs to the water, keeping their backs to us, which makes a great separation and this separation grows wider when the land needs them so much. There had been the haymaking time, now it was time for the harvest, there was the spraying of the sulfates; and, even though school was out, even the children weren't to be seen because as soon as they're eight or nine years old they start to make themselves useful. In April, in May, even in June, or at the beginning of June, it's different: then the weather turns fine, calling you out into the sainfoins and the flowering clover and it's like a sunset in front of the sickle that goes round and round; out toward the native red wheat and the special wheat; out toward the vines that have any downy mildew, any oidium, any worms; up to the tops of the hill and in the lowest fields and in the pastures and even in the orchards having a beehive or two, aside from a great number of cherry trees against which we'll have to place a long ladder. At the very limit, on Sunday or Saturday night, or after a particularly wearying day, the boys go swimming with the other boys and the girls go swimming with the other girls. When Rouge was making his rounds, he only met with some hikers, people just walking through, from far away—strangers. In the end, he was reassured.

Anyway, she was there, and that was what counted. The girl, she is there and she is with us; the rest matters very little. He looks again to see if she is really there, then maybe he has nothing to do but keep calm, because one shouldn't ask too much. He kept himself perfectly calm for several days; it was raining. Again, we see storms hanging over the lake like bed sheets hanging perfectly vertical. The sky was extinguished. The girl was extinguished as well. She was no longer shining. She had become all gray. One day she is shining, then she shines no more. She took refuge in her little black dress where she kept herself still, putting her chin in her hand, then her elbow on her knee, in front of the rain. The sky hid its lovely colors so well that one wonders if it will find them ever again, because it had to reinvent itself on its own. And the girl, maybe she's also finished, because she had invented herself as well (or maybe we were inventing her). Now, he just has to keep calm; he comes to sit beside her; one has to kill impossible things inside oneself, he sits beside her on the bench. Because of the porch roof, we were sheltered from the rain. The big waves holding a tangled wig of grass and rotten fish in their crests left a smooth green hill of debris near you, before crashing over themselves with their spray. We try to guess how far up the shoreline they will go, where one will overtake another, but we can never know which will go the farthest. This one is going to touch the tip of my sole, we think, and then it doesn't at all. The smallest ones often have the best chance. The third one, leaving the shoreline, for example: "Juliette, shall we bet?" It's like a horse race. She said, "I choose the fourth one." The game seemed to amuse her. And maybe nothing more, ever again, but to be like that, the two of them, and watching how the high water breaks their bottles of thick green glass, their Bordeaux, whose shards rattle against the worn stones around you. And over there, they're firing the cannon. Boom! They've got two or three cannons on the hillside; they've numbered them; so "Cannon Number One, Fire!... Number Two, Fire!" It echoes as well toward Denens and Redenges on the other side of the village, but a bit muted, with less power, like when Chauvy shows up too late at the old woman's house where we've put him to lodge and he kicks the base of the door. From Milliquet's, you could hear it well. Already at nine o'clock everything was closed up at the old lady's; and him, then, banging with his fists first, then his feet against the door; but the woman behind the shutters said, "Bang away, go on, you've got time, that'll teach you..." And so the waves amidst the sound of broken glass, while they're firing the cannon, and thus the waves toward Redenges; and maybe it will be all there is, forever, maybe he'll never have another thing; but at least she's there, and he finds her next to him. So he showed her a spot in the sky where there was a hole like one made through a wall for a window when the bits of rock are uneven.

"Well," he said. "Juliette... Juliette," he said, "here comes the nice weather... the wind has started moving again up there."

We saw her raise her head, looking through the bit of hand he'd held out to see the clouds like pieces of rock, black or slate colored, brown and riddled with gray, crossing over each other, then falling together against the mountain like a rock slide. She sees there is a great battle raging in the sky and that the sky is continually transforming itself. Down here, the wind comes against your face and your body in great soft bursts, in little air bubbles it pushes forward with its two hands; but up there... and, in fact, Rouge said, "Tomorrow it will be fine... and that will make you happy, won't it? Rain doesn't suit you so much, Juliette. It makes you sad..."

He stands up, he walks a few steps around the house, inspecting everything as usual, but there is still no one. There is only Décosterd who thought he'd take advantage of the occasion.

"Listen, boss, the weather will be good tomorrow... what if we went fishing? I'm wondering if the fish are missing me as much as I'm missing them... in any case, the nets are thirsty and that's not good for them..."

He was thinking he'd better try to distract him a little.

And Rouge said, "Yes, why not after all? Tomorrow or the next day, better yet the day after tomorrow, if you want..."

Only it was the day after tomorrow that the old man arrived (and so we didn't go fishing that day or the next, nor any of the days that followed).

The little old man had a gray shirt (he was both the court clerk and the forest warden); he had a thick cloth shirt and an unstarched but very clean collar; blue linen trousers, a yellow straw hat like a Panama, folded back at the front.

"I've got a convocation for you, Mr. Rouge."

Under his arm was a fishing rod with guides, there to witness his professional duties.

And Rouge said, "A convocation?"

"Yes, a convocation from the Judge… it's about this inquiry."

"What inquiry?"

"The inquiry that was opened following Mr. Milliquet's complaint… for corruption of a minor…"

Rouge said, "Oh!" His face puffed as if someone was strangling him. "Oh… okay, okay… when is it?"

"Next Wednesday."

The little old man fished the paper from a special pocket his wife had sewn inside his shirt: To Jules Rouge, fisherman…Wednesday 11 August at 10 o'clock…

"Oh," Rouge said again. Then the fat vein he had on the side of his neck jumped. "And so what? You too! You…."

But already Décosterd was holding him back by his arm; and, without getting upset (it's because he was used to it), the little old man said, "What's the fuss, Mr. Rouge? We're just doing our job. And remind yourself that it isn't only a piece of paper… not just one more paper."

All the hunchback had to do then was go to Juliette. He said to her, "Would you like to take a little walk?"

He had come that day in the afternoon; all he had to do was take advantage of Rouge's trip into the village; and when Juliette tipped her head toward Décosterd, he said, "Oh, don't worry… I'll explain everything to you, but not here, because this isn't where we belong."

"Where do we belong?"

"You'll see."

The hunchback speaks a strange language, she has trouble understanding him.

He had a hard time getting up from amidst the flat stones and pieces of pink tile; he puts the strap of his instrument over his shoulder; the first thing he'd done was pick up his instrument.

She had gone into her room; she reappeared, she changed her dress, she has a little black shawl over her shoulders.

Décosterd still looked like he hadn't noticed, Décosterd appeared not to see them, Décosterd had his back to them.

To their right were the drawings on the water made by the choppy wind, like a lady opening her fan, a big silk fan covered in silver sparkles. Nature doesn't bother about them, they don't bother any part of the nature. They went between the reeds like going between two walls of vines, painted gray at the bottom, painted green at the top; the reeds aren't shocked, the reeds weren't bothered. She was walking in front, he was behind. He had two humps. The narrowness of the path made it so he had to put his accordion on his back; and so it was another hump on the first hump. They were able to go out into nature where they don't bother anyone, except we hear a frog jump into its pond from time to time, and they arrived near the boats where she stops, but Urbain shook his head: we're not yet where we belong. He points to the cliff. The instrument is in its case that buttons along the side. So she looks at him, then she points to the water in front of them; she laughs. It's lovely clear water, because the cloudy brown water that had come during the rain had vanished with the good weather. It's lovely clear water filled with big gold coins or at least they looked like gold coins, these light yellow leaves on the bottom like the kind that fall from the poplars in the fall. Oh, it feels good here amidst these things, but, you, how will you manage to get across? Because this water is deeper than one foot, but that doesn't really stop me, doesn't bother me, hiking up her skirt, now it was hiked; and he stayed alone on the shoreline like Rouge had done another time, while the water rose above her knee. Turning her head from time to time, she moves forward through the circles that spread out around her, that cross over one another, that get all mixed up together; and the little waves hit against one another and they clap, while she is laughing again, turning her head to the hunchback. She breaks all the images that are reflected in the lovely mirror: a shrub, a tuft of grass, the sandy hillside, the sky; and a pine tree hangs still in the mirror, then it disappears in black ribbons that fray into nothing. Earthbound things, all the lovely things of the earth, and she is among them and they disappear; then here they return one after another, and each takes its place yet again. She made a sign to the hunchback over the things that came back, beneath a slice of blue sky. All he has to do is walk up the shoreline from where he's standing; the girl, she goes up from where she is to the place where the river can be walked across. Several kingfishers take flight, making a blue streak through the air, just where the light hits it, and then it is a black streak. He walks beneath his two humps, his head forward; he slips into the black earth. We can hear again the water of the river coming with the things she says, because here the water doesn't speak, further upstream the water speaks. He is among the tufts of swamp grass and the big wild celery blooms with their stems filled with juice that explode beneath his feet, making him stumble. But she heads in his direction. Again, she walks toward him with her beautiful legs, moving toward him from rock to rock; she held out her hand to him. She says, "You wanted to take me for a walk, but I'm the one leading us," because he has trouble with his oversized head, his skinny, too-short legs; he struggles to cross the water and he struggles after he's crossed, and after that he struggles even more. They are on the rise of the cliff, between the little rock walls. Again and again, she took him by the arm on the steep hill, between the thorny bushes filled with big green grasshoppers and others that turn blue and red when they take flight into the sunshine. And so they found themselves again at the water, but above it now, at a significant height above the lake and just where the cliff overhung—jutting toward this warm cinder. Because it isn't yet where we belong, not exactly where we belong, as the hunchback had said; but here was the little alcove again, which appeared before them suddenly, settled into a half-circle in the still steep hillside, beneath a crown of tall pine trees. And, behind you, all the things from before were removed, one after the other, sliding rapidly to the side and disappearing: this mountain, the setting sun, the pine trees along the shoreline, the shoreline, the pine tree forest;—all this slides away and vanishes, and Décosterd mending his nets, and the house and then even the shoreline itself; because they were turning, they turned, and there, the hunchback said, "We're here."

They sat down. The terraced ground formed little benches that were covered with a little dry grass on which was blooming a kind of dandelion with bright yellow petals; they sat down on one of these benches. They could see no one, here they bother no one and no one bothers them. All that was in front of them was the breadth of the water, which was empty, which was smooth like the floorboard of a room, while the overhang of the cliff made it so they were completely separated from the world on either side of them. Nothing but three or four leagues of water in front of you and nothing on the water but a little white sail. Beneath them and around their feet was a kind of mossy swamp made by a spring that ran from the base of the cliff; the spring fed into the lake through a marshy area planted with willows. There, just as they'd arrived they'd heard frogs jumping into the water again, and that was all. He sits down, he brought his accordion to his knees; he unbuttons it tenderly, exposing the lovely red bellows to the air, then he plays a C, and then C sharp... He rests his cheek on one of the flat sides of the instrument; he plays a scale, then another.

He spoke a strange language. It was like he couldn't speak unless he'd first got his accordion playing and played it. Here there are only good things to see, good things to hear; we don't bother them and we are not bothered by them. And this is what he said, this is how he started to speak in his strange language, but we could hear him easily because of the music that came before he spoke and comes while he's speaking and came after, because his music is laughter, or then it's scolding, or then it rushes or sighs, or says, "Too bad." And it is happy or unhappy, or it even teases or is surprised.

He says, "Down there, we've been bothering..."

The music played through a little scale that takes off, rising toward the forest where it tricks a bird, waking it up.

"There was no place for you down there..."

This is what he said: he brought forward a great chord to underline and highlight the thought:

"No place for me, either..."

And the same chord was played.

We see that he still has the same pale little head, the same skinny, hairless cheeks, with a little blue at his temples, an overly thin and heavily corded neck; and, on his hands, we see plenty of little cords tight beneath his skin:

"No place, no, no place... no place for you, no place for me."

And then he goes on, he goes on anyway; but then, a place for us, will it be here?

The music says no.

It will be far, very far, says the music, which goes further and further in a neverending line:

"And so," he said, "we've got to go... stay for this coming Sunday, and we'll leave the one after that..."

He plays a little march, with a fanfare like soldiers on the roads:

"You and me... because we can't... we can't stay here... And now listen... It's Décosterd..."

He doesn't know how to pronounce the name, he starts again two or three times:

"Yes, Décosterd... he explained everything to me when he brings me home at night, because they're afraid for me... And they're afraid for you, too, they're afraid of Rouge for you..."

His fingers went along the keys.

"They don't want you to stay at Rouge's because the police would come to take you away from there. And so they want you to leave, but they want to keep you all the same."

While his fingers keep playing, "They don't want to make you leave for you, they want to make you leave for them..."

The music laughs again and now there are two birds tricked up above them, now three or four, even if it isn't even the season:

"These are your friends, they would like to keep you close to them. They asked me to help them, they think I'm going to help them. There will be a party, yes, eight days from now on Sunday the 15th... they told me to bring you. They say they'll arrange it so Rouge won't see you leaving, and once you're there... I told them yes... you understand why... I told them yes and they're counting on me... And

I'll bring you and they think they'll take you from there; but, I'm going to pack my things, and you, you'll pack your things, and we'll go off into the world..."

This is what he says beneath the gilded ferns, beneath the beautiful flowers of the peach tree, through the great red leather bellows: an instrument with twelve bass notes and keys made of silver:—she looks around her into the world, and the music will go forward.

She raised her head, without having moved her hands; and without having looked at him, she looks forward: we'll go out into the world, we'll bother no one, no one will bother us.

A smile comes to him. We don't bother the birds here, just the opposite; the birds believe they're among other birds. We hear the chaffinch, which we've tricked, and as soon as the tune finishes, the bird takes it up and answers; or the warbler or the chickadee. We'll go out into the world: we'll make the birds sing.

She had begun to smile; slowly the smile overcame her face and she finally turned toward him:

"It's just that my uncle has my papers..."

But he laughs, the accordion laughs, and up above the warbler is laughing too, along with the chaffinch and the chickadee.

"And it's just that I have no money."

But he only races his fingers more quickly across the keys.

And the music changed its rhythm slowly beneath his fingers; the birds above, the two or three birds quiet down because they hear the music changing: the warblers above, the chaffinches, the chickadees.

There was a little pause, on purpose, and there was a mistake in the notes, on purpose; then it was like running out of breath, then it swung; he shuffled from one foot to the other, without changing place, with breaks and like a pause: does she understand?

He takes one hand from the keys (while the other is still playing); he removes his hat, then he places it next to him.

She understands a little better, she doesn't yet understand completely: so, his hand returns to the keys, his hand leaves them again. He picks up a stone, he throws it into the hat.

And the rhythm explodes;—two stones, then three stones and four; this is how we'll go out into the world... And you...

He had no need to add a thing; she stood up. There is only a tiny space up here, not much bigger than the top of a table, but one doesn't need a bigger space, just as we will see, because often (over there, where we're from), the top of a table is all we need.

He watches, he sees that it works. A hat on the ground, the music.

And he goes forward with his rhythm, then we hear a little wave coming like the sound of applause.

Everything is in harmony.

Now he's stopped; so she looks at him. We see again how pale he is, how the sweat drips from his forehead. There is a wet lock of hair over it and atop the thick vein. He leans forward with his skinny neck, he breathes hard. She watches him, then she comes (because when we've given one thing, maybe we have to give it all); she sits close to him, drops her shawl beside her on the sand; stretches out her arm, leans over.

She leans to the left, which is the side of the greatest weight, then stretches her arm, her lovely bare arm, so soft and round, and strong (if we needed it to be); stretches it out and goes to the weak little back, slides up, searching for the neck.

But he jerks his head; he moves away from her, he moves away.

A frog jumps into its pond.

We'll go together, that's all. Everything must be where it belongs, and each of us where we belong.

She sees that he's right. A frog jumps into its pond.

XII

So the next to last Sunday came (because the last one didn't count).

That day Bolomey had been fishing all morning, even if it was illegal to fish on Sundays, but the fish warden was a friend of his. In the afternoon, he put on his big plastic boots that go all the way up to mid-thigh; he put on his khaki vest with its metal buttons in the shape of boars' heads. He went up the Bourdonnette. He went as far as the train viaduct with its great stone arches that traverse the entire width of the valley, and the river passes between two of the pillars. Bolomey stopped beneath the viaduct. He leans against the stone. He looks up, straight out toward the stone, a flat line like he'd held out a yardstick, his glance rises up, tracing the blue stones stacked one atop the other in their cement frame; then straight up against the construction which goes a little backward and behind up the hill, so straight that finally one's glance shifts just to be in the air; and Bolomey was looking at the empty sky, because there wasn't even the slightest cloud. And just then a train passed, but we couldn't see it, neither could Bolomey; the train only made its noise, an unsituated noise, an elsewhere kind of noise that is everywhere and nowhere, that filled the sky without us being able to say from where it came, nor where it's going: like the start of a storm, like an approaching hailstorm: then suddenly the noise stopped... It was Décosterd who had promised. Décosterd would take care of Rouge. While the rest of us would take care of her... Bolomey stopped staring at the pillar, because he'd only studied it to work out its height: maybe thirty meters. He didn't even have his fishing rod; he's here instead to see what's happening, because they told me, "Keep a watch near the quarry and along the Bourdonnette." Okay. He wet his boots in the deep water. He walks down with the current. We could hear that it was a Sunday. The train's little storm had quieted for a moment already; Bolomey was walking back down the river beneath the pine tree forest. And we could hear yelling up above; there are voices shouting up above, or singing; a Sunday with Sunday strollers, while there are those out hunting mushrooms in their secret spots, looking for bolets (which is what we call them) or chanterelles.

He arrived below his house. There we see him walk back up the hill. He went inside his house. He takes the key to the front door from his pocket, he opens the door.

Sunday, a beautiful August Sunday, the second Sunday of August; the goings-on of Sunday were going along their peaceful way, with a bit of the world and something unexpected from time to time. And so, up there, the voices continued, women's voices, children's voices, men's voices, all in a great peacefulness; nevertheless, Bolomey goes into his house and when he came back out, we see that his rifle is on his shoulder. We're in with the game warden, and we can go out with our rifle four or five weeks before the season opens without having any trouble; anyway, we'll tell him what it's all about. We'll tell him: "You, you've got your revolver… it's still this Savoyard. Go take a look, if you want, near the quarry; me, I'll go toward Rouge's house…" Bolomey, his rifle on his shoulder, climbs up the moss and the black earth. He heads over toward the cliff beneath the pine trees. He climbs the hill, having avoided the most commonly-used areas; he arrives beneath the pine trees to the outcroppings from where we see Rouge's house and its tri-colored roof. Just there, the water comes to meet you in its reflections along the length of the tree trunks and its white fires above you in the branches, like the glint of a raised pickaxe, the glint of the downward thrust, the glint going up, the glint going down. We would like to see a little what's happening near Rouge's house and there is no better place than here, as little Maurice knew very well, when he came to this exact spot and lay down in the bushes. Bolomey comes here as well; the light off the water hits him square in the face. The light hits you, walking across you like opening and closing a window in the sun. Bolomey puts his hand across his eyes; he watches between his fingers, at the same time he slips into the thorny bushes and into the ones that make little purple husk-shaped seeds that dry-out quickly; he can now take his hand off his eyes, and we see the house come into view (it's more of a shed) with its tri-colored roof and set right into the worn stones, and there is still no one before the door. Further along the shoreline, two older girls are holding hands with a small child who is learning to walk:—but all the same we see that there is an entire preparation happening on this next-to-last Sunday (because the last one will not count) out on the water. On the water, in the air, across the entire sky, and also over there opposite you, from the peak to the base of the mountain; it's shining, it's clean, all is remade new: all these rocks, these pastures, these forests, these grasslands, these fields, seen like beneath a glass. The water, even the water has been polished; the water, even more care was put into the water for this next-to-last Sunday, so much so that the other shore can be seen twice, the entire mountain exists on two planes; and we steer around the upturned peak of the Dent d'Oche, in the boat we are suspended halfway up the upturned rocks of the Meillerie; we are in a boat and at the same time in a mountain gondola, one of those buckets that slide along a cable above a gorge. Bolomey understands: everything has been made beautiful one last time for her, and it's to tell her goodbye. All the villages are shown in double; it's for her. And we see in double the red or brown spots made by the villages and the straw-colored squares where the harvest has just finished. Bolomey has understood; so he looks around a little again at what's happening, but nothing worrying is going on, which is why he hides his rifle beneath a ridge of sandstone to keep it dry until he comes back for it; after which, he went back down the hill. He entered the path between the reeds.

It was this next-to-last Sunday; neither Rouge nor Décosterd nor the girl had been fishing any of the preceding days. For all this time, the same net had been left out to dry between the drying poles, and it was all sun bleached, all "cindered" as Décosterd called it. It had become white as ash, even if when these same nets are used they are blue like the sky, light green like young grass, they are golden like honey.

The nets were no longer being used and hadn't been used for quite some time, something which Bolomey quickly noticed. It was just as he arrived in front of Rouge's house. Rouge was sitting on the bench and Juliette was talking to him. Décosterd, he was cleaning up the dishes in the kitchen. Bolomey sees that Juliette was talking to Rouge, and Rouge didn't look happy; he was nodding his head, he was saying, "But is it safe, Juliette?"

Just then he sees that Bolomey is there; so he turned toward him, he starts, "What do you think, Bolomey? She'd like to take a little tour with the boat…"

"Why not?" said Bolomey.

"You know exactly what's going on."

"Nothing at all is going on," said Bolomey, "no need to worry, I came here from my rounds."

But Rouge continues to nod his head. He wasn't wearing his nice suit. He was wearing old leather slippers without a heel; on his feet were pink cotton socks. He shakes his head. He puts his elbows on his knees.

And nevertheless, over there, everything kept on calling to you; two villages instead of one were calling you and it's the same village. Two mountain peaks and no longer one, two walls of rock shining like sheets of white iron, because she is not yet there. The wind had completely fallen; the heat was growing stronger and stronger on the sand, on the soft stones, and on the bench even if it was made of wood: on the water which was beginning to steam with white. We were hearing singing from up on the cliff where the families must have been settled in front of the beautiful view, and now everyone's curiosity was brought to the other side of the shore, while out in the middle of the lake, and coming toward you, there was a great black boat beneath two high crossed sails. And the girl, in the end, she couldn't ignore it, even when Rouge kept saying "no" from the bench; we saw her stand up. Bolomey kept himself seated next to Rouge on the bench. Rouge was no longer talking. His arms crossed over his knees, he puffed on his extinguished pipe.

It's this next-to-last Sunday; the weather had never been so fine. Over there, we see them running on the boat, bringing the base of the sails back in; the one at the rudder pushes against the bar with all the strength in his back. They were leaning the whole time to the side, going sometimes from east to west, sometimes west to east, parallel to the shoreline so they could study it and examine it carefully each time. It was after they had played cards and before they'd started playing cards again; but now they were seated along the edge of the boat. The great black shell twisted below them like a snake cut in half, a snake that was thicker than a thigh, and the sails were like puddles of white starch. Facing the shore, they could see the whole beautiful scene; it was offered up to them from its start to its finish, with each stage. They saw quickly that it grew more lively very fast.

Big Alexis had gone to get his horse from the stable after removing his vest and his collar; Maurice was positioned again on the cliff. We see big Alexis come down the path that followed the Bourdonette, seated on his great red horse, his dragon horse riddled with nerves and veins beneath the skin, and whose well-brushed coat shines like a roof washed with rain. All the beautiful things of the earth are there, and, the men, they were all there too: Bolomey, Maurice whom we cannot see, Alexis on his big horse, Chauvy with his little cane, all while the mountain gave its salute. And now Alexis, keeping his horse with one hand, removes his shoes in the reeds, meaning that he'd passed his right arm through the bridle and calmed his horse with his voice. The preacher's harmonium had finished two or three canticles this morning, up toward the high vault of the trees, in front of God's handiwork;—here, he gets barefoot while the animal shows the brand at his throat made by the military authorities. All the frogs jumped into the water. Madeleine, Marie and Hortense had gone into the forest to see where they might find the most beautiful moss when it comes time to make their garlands, and it won't be long now. Now Alexis hides his shoes in the reeds, then removes his white shirt, and the hair on his forehead was curly and the hair on his chest was curly. "Hold on! Hold on! Artagnan, a little patience... what are you doing? Softly now..." The animal with its great milky blue eyes abruptly reared back, goes forward, turns its twitching rump sideways and the skin riddles like water beaten with wind: "Steady! Steady! Softly now, Artagnan…"

From where they were seated on the hot sand, they could see the entire boat. And when she appeared, they saw her, too; they were the first to see her when she showed herself in the reeds. Everything was waiting for her and finally there she was; she comes, she comes forth a last time; and at first she pushes her boat out toward the middle of the lake. Everything was waiting for her, she goes forward. Rouge had not raised his head, having only slid his glance toward her from beneath his big eyebrows; at the most he made a movement with his hands and we saw an aluminum ring slip onto his little finger. But she was still going forward, going forward with a great rhythmic movement of her entire body on the rippled water; then she drops the oars…

Rouge was the only one who wasn't watching, because now everything watches her. Up the lake, big Alexis had climbed back atop his horse: the hooves hit the sand, hit the mud, hit the water; with great thrusts of his heels, he pushes his horse forward to see better (or is it to be better seen?) We are watching from up on the cliff, we are watching from the boat, we are watching from the shoreline, we are watching from our seat on the bench. And, the girl, the girl stood up slowly, she has turned toward us, she has waved to us. Bolomey answered her. Rouge didn't answer her. Rouge has not moved and his head is still hung forward. She turned toward us, then she turned again toward the mountain, while we see her raise her arms; we see her arms move up against the lovely blue hillside, up until they have touched the rocks. And a great lovely movement raced up her body, like a wave rising up and pushing against another wave; along her legs, along her sides, over her back, atop her shoulders;—after which everything vanished, everything disappeared, everything was extinguished.

The great black kite, who, in search of food, has left his high-altitude journey on the plateau has had enough time to descend in a series of circles. He touched the water with the tip of his wing, trying to take a dead fish from the surface of the water with his claw; he rose up in a diagonal line; his claw is empty: he missed his fish. Everything is empty; this is when she was no longer there. This is while they were steering toward us again in their great black boat with an eye forward, while Alexis pressed into his horse with his naked heels trying to make it go into the deep water; everything was empty, everything was extinguished; and then everything is set alight again.

She reappeared; she was coming out of the water. Everything is set alight and comes alive, while the animal farther up the shore recoils and while the water, in a great upheaval, breaks into a million pieces around her.

The sun lights up his curly-haired chest as it heaves, rising up then falling back, and along his sides are two shadows...

She reappeared, she rises up little by little, she was born again before us. Slowly, once again, she raised her body, she gave it form and substance in the air: it was like her body gave meaning to everything. It seems that everything was suddenly crowned, and that this crowning gave an explanation for everything, and suddenly everything expresses itself, then, having been expressed, everything will quiet again; everything will quiet again, alas! Forever. The girl, she laughed again in our direction—then, in fact, because nothing lasts on the earth, because nowhere does beauty have its place for very long...

It was the men on the boat. They had their dinghy they used to go to the shore when they had thrown anchor in the deep. One of them had started to run toward the back of the boat. He brought the dinghy to him using the rope by which it was attached like a pony to its mother. He jumps in the dinghy; the others are already laughing.

And everything is ruined further still or in another way, because then we saw Rouge, who had not yet moved, stand up abruptly.

He goes into his house, he came out quickly; something was shining in his hands. Then: bang!... bang!...

The two shots had followed each other so quickly that the air hadn't had enough time to settle between the first and the second; a first upheaval in the air that heaves again in the middle of its upheaval; then, three times each, the two shots smacked against the cliff, against the forest, into the ravine and resounded against one another.

Later in the evening, we saw two policemen go by in their full uniforms.

There was no longer anyone on the shoreline. Rouge's house was shuttered.

The noises from the villages were further on. Even the waves were keeping quiet here, all the water and all the air. It was after Juliette had rowed quickly back to shore, while Rouge's shotgun was still smoking between the two barrels; the young man in his dinghy had stopped rowing. The girl, she had jumped onto the shore; Décosterd had just enough time to pull the boat toward him before it was pulled back out toward the middle of the lake.

He'd rowed it back to its buoy without a word; when he got back to the house, Bolomey was gone.

And he would have liked to stay, but Rouge said, "Oh, we'll be fine on our own; I know what I've got to do now. You see, it isn't difficult... if anyone comes back to bother me..."

He shows Décosterd the shotgun.

Then he looked at Décosterd sideways, in a way he'd never done before. "We don't need you, go on... you understand?"

He repeated, "You understand?" looking at Décosterd sideways, with anger and impatience; so Décosterd had thought it best not to cross him that night, because he could always keep an eye on things from afar...

For now everything is deeply silent. Even the waves keep quiet here and all the water is silent and the air, while the sky is all yellow, then it became all pink. Rouge had coughed a little in the kitchen, the policemen were long gone. The water was yellow, then the water was green and pink, then only pink; he coughs once, he placed his hand in front of his mouth. He looks at his worn old leather slippers, his ribbed cotton socks. He goes to knock on Juliette's door. No answer. "Oh, well," he said, "it's like that." He lights the oil lamp that he'd set on the pinewood table covered with an oil cloth depicting the Battle of Bourget (and everywhere there is war, but we won't let ourselves be pushed around).

What an ungrateful girl.

He'd hung up the shotgun on a nail in his room; he goes to get it, grabs it by both barrels, and comes back with the gun, settling it before him beneath the lamp. The Battle of Bourget, battle everywhere. With the little pot of oil, the stick, the cloths to put around the stick, and it's true isn't it? Haven't we done everything we could for her?

The Bavarians had raupen helmets, the naval riflemen had berets with pompoms. It was the naval riflemen who were attacking, commanded by an officer wearing an admiral's uniform with insignia. Rouge grabbed his gun again, set it down across his knees; the cross at the top of the cloth shows the officer raising his sword, while the

Bavarians are leaving by the postern, on top of which were dogs, because this was an old shotgun with a hammer in the shape of a dog's head. Higher up, in the glacis, the explosion of a mortar made a white circle which was surrounded with a crown of smoke. Rouge, putting his weapon across his knees... and its true, because she has everything or she could have everything; his weapon across his knees on the cloth of his trousers: a room for her, furniture for her, linens for her, a boat for her, a part of the house for her, the entire house if she wanted it... we refused her nothing, we would refuse her nothing. It's true, or isn't it? He looks in front of him, but, over to the right the events are interrupted by the light from the lamp hanging from its brass chain, the print erased and the plaster fallen in this spot... So? So, it's like we've done nothing... We hadn't used this table cloth in a long time; Décosterd found it folded up at the bottom of the cupboard, and he'd said, "It's still good..." which meant that the officer was now raising his arm again and the raupen helmet of the Bavarian who was being bayoneted in his stomach had started to fall again. He'd been falling all this time since the battle, meaning from the battle of 1870, this war before the big war, but just below his helmet there was a hole... Just when everything was coming together so nicely... All she had to do was want it too, when all seemed to have been arranged just for her and she wouldn't have been more at home anywhere else (exactly because we needed women, we've always needed more women...) the repairs, the construction, making everything new, the painting... He had pushed the stick into the barrel, having placed his weapon upright between his legs, having rolled the cloths around the stick, having covered them first with oil.

It's for the others if they want to come, but they saw how

we'll welcome them... For the others, just in case they're
tempted to come back, those who come on their feet in
groups of two, and me, I'm just one and I'm alone, but
we'll count for two at least... this battle at Bourget was
bothering him. The Bavarian's helmet just wouldn't fall. He
pumped the stick up and down while seated astride the
bench; into one barrel and then the other, then he says, to
sum it all up "Anyway, I'm sixty-two-years old. I could be
her grandfather. And yet here, we have our freedom. And
anyway she would have been made for this life, since she
already knows how to fish or mostly... Oh, if only she
wanted..." He listens, turned to the side, and listens with
all the power of his ear toward the door that has still not
opened, that isn't even ajar, behind which still nothing
happens; so his anger moved from his head into his
shoulder, coursing along his arms which were still pumping
up and down, because after all it isn't his fault; and the
Bourget still hasn't been taken, but it's because of... and
well, they'll get what's coming to them! The barrels, then
the hammer, and everything must be carefully cleaned and
polished, then two shotgun shells, then we make a hole in
the shutters or we'll stand behind the planks in the shed;
we've still got about ten days to ourselves and then we'll see
them coming; and then... his hands fall. He lets the end of
the stick drop to the floor. We hear nothing from where
we're listening into; it's like we're beyond this world. He
sets the gun on the table. He's going to see if the front
door to the house is closed. He came back, he sat back
down. He struggles to sort all these things in his mind.
Today, Milliquet, the judge, the clerk, the bailiff, the
policemen, an inquiry, then a verdict; and they are the
world, they are outside; us, here, we're beyond the world. It
will be a week, a week and three or four days. So he
thought some more, he struggles to think between his

eyebrows drawn together with the effort of his thinking; and then she hears him calling her name, in the evening of this next-to-last Sunday (the last did not count); she had thrown herself fully dressed across her bed, she hadn't lit her lamp; and he, picking up his weapon, goes to hang it on its nail.

She hears him say, "You sleeping, Juliette?"

"No."

"Oh, good. Because I've got to speak to you." He says, "I've a proposition... maybe you'll agree."

He had gone to the door and held his hand toward the doorknob, but he brings it back to him abruptly, and he even takes a step backward.

He sees the table then; he sees the lovely quiet of the light of the table lamp beneath its white porcelain shade with its brass ring; he walks a bit further, he pulls the bench toward him; and she hears him speaking:

"Because we're going to have to decide..."

She had brought the covers up over her body. The stars shone through the curtains, making it possible to see in the room or at least to see what was white, a strip of wall, the bed, the furniture. The girl, we couldn't have seen her right away. The girl, she existed only in the background because she still wasn't moving; only her voice marked her presence, while this other voice came through the door. The girl, she had said, "No," and outside, he had said, "Well, good..."

Then he says, "Because we're going to have to decide... do you want to go back to Milliquet's?"

"Ah, so you don't?"

"Only, if you don't go back to his house... the state is going to take care of you... they'll send you somewhere. They'll send policemen to get you... you didn't see the ones who came earlier." She hadn't seen them. "So, you didn't see them, well, I certainly saw them…"

He starts again, "Does that mean anything to you?"

And then he said, "Juliette, come here please."

Overcome with a need to stand up, he holds himself with both hands on the table—to keep himself from getting up:

"I would like to speak with you seriously, it's the last chance, you know… I've a proposition. Juliette, Juliette, if only you wanted… we've got money… Juliette!"

He listens and nothing comes, nothing moves.

"Juliette, are you there?"

"Yes…"

He gets up again, he goes toward the door. Suddenly, he stops, his hands hang from his body, he raised a hand, his hand falls again; he puts it into his pocket, he puts the other hand into his other pocket.

And he stood there for another instant, then begins to turn in a circle.

He says, "Money and a boat, that's enough."

She answers yes, then no, then yes; then no; that's all. He told her to come, she didn't come; but we've got money, Juliette, we've got the boat… the boat named after you…

"Listen, next Sunday there'll be the Fleur-de-Lys party. And they'll leave us alone until then… the verdict won't come in until three days after that, at the earliest. And, next Sunday, everyone will be at the party. We'll just have to wait until nighttime; no one will see us leave. Décosterd will even be at the party, and surely the hunchback, too."

He was turning in a circle, he was turning around the table; he stopped, then started again:

"So you pack up your things and we'll take your boat, Juliette. We'll get out of here, no one will notice a thing, no one will know where we are... we'll cross the water... we'll cross the water and over there it's another country and they can't do anything to us... we'll stay there until... until you're of age, yes, and it's only a few months anyway. So you decide. Because I'll adopt you. If you'd like... you'll be my daughter, anyway I had no child, I had no wife, nor a child... And over there, in the Savoy, we could always continue working while we wait; I'll write a word to Décosterd so he'll take care of the house. It's only three hours crossing. So are we understood or what?"

Because she was no longer saying a thing, but he must have thought she had no need to say anything else; he continued:

"Nothing easier than that. So, okay, you pack up your things. We'll cross the water, it will be better... here, I would have done something terrible..."

He was standing, his hands in his pockets:

"Yes, I would have done something terrible and we're not the strongest... but don't say anything to anyone... now you should sleep."

Then he said one more thing:

"Good night."

XIII

There were three of them: Madeleine, Marie and Hortense; there were three girls with two baskets.

They were going up above the ravine of the Bourdonnette beneath the big pine trees, and from time to time, getting down on their knees, they pulled at the moss that then came away in sheets. It was Friday night. They were pulling at the sheets of moss, then arranging the sheets flat into the bottom of the baskets which they picked up by the handle; but sometimes the tree trunks were too close together and forced them walk one after another, while elsewhere it was not so and they grew at a great distance from each other with their enormous columns on which a white bead dripped like a candle that is burning badly. We are gathering moss for the garlands and we are only three girls and no boys, because the boys were all kept back at the Fleur-de-Lys with nails to hammer and metal wires to stretch out.

Below the girls was the sound of the water. Just beside them began the lovely green and red hillside, with its carpet of needles on the ledges, its little rock walls; and hanging here and there is more moss, but it hangs and so isn't the right kind. It's moss like a man's beard, sometimes white, sometimes yellow, not the green moss we're looking for. So they walked along the edge of the ravine without going down it, leaning over and then straightening, and all three together and then one by one, then they call out to each other laughing.

Abruptly, they quieted.

It was just as they came back to their baskets which were nearly full; Marie said, "Did you hear that?"

At the base of the ravine, from amidst the sound of the water, came another sound; it was like someone walking on a dry branch, and the branch breaks, then a stone moves across another stone with a scratching sound.

"Did you hear that?"

People say these woods are filled with bandits. People tell about the story of the Savoyard and Juliette (you know, Milliquet's niece who is now at Rouge's house because Milliquet threw her out); and it seems she's got to come to the party Sunday...

"It can't be!"

"Yes, she's invited..."

Then Marie said again, "Did you hear that?" and then all three of them moved backward so they were hidden by the edge of the hillside.

It was below them, they stretched their necks: we saw the leaves shake on the alders that grew like a curtain on the other side of the river; and suddenly Marie said, "Look!"

She points at a straw hat that has appeared between the leaves, appeared then disappeared; but then she says in a different voice:

"Hey! Mister..."

She steps forward, she leans over the hill, she calls, "Hey, Mister!"

She yells louder and the two others join in.

"Hey, Mister! Mister!"

They get no answer. The alder leaves hang still.

The hat can no longer be seen.

She laughed.

"Maybe he's German?"

And while the other two pull her back, she yells, "Hey! Mein Herr..."

And nothing. So, "He's English. Hey! Sir!"

We speak three languages when we want, but it seems none of the three was understood. So we leave again, heads down beside the alders, beneath their shade; and the hat can no longer be seen; so now Marie turns to us and says:

"You didn't see who it was? Well! You didn't recognize him? ... It was Maurice, Maurice Busset. He's the only one with..."

"Where is he going like that?"

"Well, where he goes!"

"And Emilie?"

"Oh, Emilie..."

So they all three look at each other, then Marie shrugged her shoulders.

They were talking a great deal. The three girls were talking in low voices and very quickly.

"Well, yes, it's like that... and Maurice told her via Décosterd that they were waiting for her... it's the hunchback who has to bring her, Juliette... the little Italian worker, you know, because he goes often to Rouge's and he plays the accordion..."

"For who?"

"For her."

"So they're coming?"

"Yes, they're coming. They're both coming and the boys came to some agreement."

"My God! What are they going to do?"

"No one knows exactly, but you just have to ask Maurice or big Alexis."

"Oh, sure, that'd be a welcome question…"

They were speaking a great deal, their teeth were shining. They were walking along with their baskets and which they placed on the ground every once in a while; then they left again with their baskets. And little by little, we were returning to the world that comes toward you through a kind of great arch beneath which the white daylight comes to meet you with its flies, its horseflies, its bumblebees. We could already hear the hammering of the nails. We arrive in a small grove. It's an old meadow. We saw the high electric posts with their red-painted rings and the sign: RISK OF DEATH, which makes you laugh. A blackbird flew straight out in front of them, beating its wings with loud cries, and they walked a short while between two hedges that blocked the view. Then, suddenly, we've arrived. Suddenly, these great buildings stand up unevenly beneath their large patched roofs; there is a name on the biggest of these, written out in new tiles: *La Fleur-de-Lys*; and below the name there is a drawing of a fleur-de-lys. This is the town inn; in front of it stood two large linden trees; beneath the lindens were benches and tables. The girls came with their baskets. We saw them coming. The boys up on their ladders were hitting nails with their hammers; we call down to them, we say: "Oh, it's you three. Well, come on then…" The party is beginning. We saw that it was a little bit farther than the inn itself, and a little bit behind the other buildings: it was a roof held up in the air by nothing, while all around it, instead of walls, was the lovely Friday evening and the beautiful party. A landscape acting as one of the walls sits beneath each side of the roof and each side shows a different terrain. The boys were still perched up on their ladders; the girls were around the tables busy unfolding flags, sorting cardboard coats-of-arms and tissue paper roses out of their boxes. We saw that, in fact,

Maurice wasn't there, and that Emilie wasn't there either. As for him, we know now where he is, but what about her? They continued to hit their nails up on their ladders, and the three girls—Marie, Hortense, Madeleine—had arrived with the baskets, then they sat down around the baskets, meaning they were seated on the table, their legs hanging down in their brown or white stockings, and even a pair of fashionable, skin-colored stockings,—holding a length of string between their fingers, then you pull a piece of moss toward you to make a bouquet. The party is being prepared. They had just turned on the electric lights. It is silent work that we do, at least for us girls (if you don't count our tongues), but the hammer blows were loud and bothered us; which is why we have to bother those above from time to time. We were calling up to them. The lovely walls of countryside on the four sides of the dance floor were now gone; four black walls had come to take their place. And, inside the walls, we had even eaten. It's the Youth Club that invited the young ladies. They had brought bread, cheese, cold sausage, salad, and a lot of white wine in a number of glass liter bottles. We drank, ate, gave cheers. Then the boys had climbed back up on their ladders, and two or three girls had lifted the sweet-smelling green snake up to them, which was cool to the touch, still heavy with dew and whose weight made it drop down to the floor in places. The boys up above pulled on the rope; the girls raised their arms. One after another they moved closer, holding the garland out to them: so beneath the thin fabric of a white linen bodice we saw a bosom rise up, a large one, then a flatter one, followed by round arms, slender ones. It smelled like pine boughs, it smelled bitter and wet. We drank again, we gave cheers. In the great green rope hanging between the wooden pillars, we saw the little pink and yellow and white and red circles, the paper roses.

We knocked our glasses together, "To your health!" — "To yours!" It made a little noise like when the goat pulls on a clump of grass and rings his own bell. And then again we land another nail. There is one that doesn't hold, we have to replace it. About ten boys, the same amount of girls. And until after eleven o'clock. We heard eleven ring out, the village clock rang each hour so slowly; this is how it rings because it's so old. It rings the hours so slowly that you cannot help hearing them, and, so steadily is the noise that, without seeming to, it finds a space between two rings to tell you, "It's time." No way not to hear the clock. It was time to go home.

They gave each other their arms, boys and girls. They went home on each other's arms. They walked along the road. They were singing. We sing a song, then we sing another; we sing all the songs that we know. Only, when one is finished, and before we move to the next, there is always a short moment of silence, and it happened during one of those silences. One of the boys said, "Do you hear that?" Everyone was silent. We heard the accordion.

Way over there down by the lake, behind the trees and the night, and weak at first amidst the sound of the water, but it managed to come through; so they laughed:

"It's the hunchback... it's Rouge that has him come to entertain her..."

"But," they said, "She'd be better off with us..."

"If the hunchback brings her, he's going to be upstaged... we'll have Gavillet and his band, eight first-rate musicians... and he'll have to keep up his courage if he wants to compete..."

"And didn't the mayor himself," we were saying, "didn't Mr. Bussigny call the policemen after those two shots fired; only it seems that Rouge just shot into the air. The man in the dinghy, anyway, was in the wrong. Nothing else happened. Still our mayor started to get worried; he told us, 'It's about time this mess is finished.' He went to see the judge. The verdict should be ready three days after the party. Rouge and Milliquet should be heard out against each other (if they attend together, which seems unlikely) —after which, they'll tell them what decision's been made. It seems like neither will be in the right. No one thinks the girl will be returned to Milliquet because he's the one who kicked her out in the first place; and we don't think Rouge will be allowed to keep her. The only solution is to put her in an institution until she becomes an adult. Only, Rouge has said, 'If the policemen come, I'll bang it all up.' Which is why the mayor is so worried and why everyone is so curious, even more curious now that the verdict will come down soon. It's too bad the situation was allowed to get to this point, but it's just the authorities would have preferred not to have to deal with it and would have done something if they could have, which would have spared them the trouble, the letters to write, the proceedings, and God knows what other complications;—and anyway, Rouge has never done anyone wrong, and not the girl either, quite the opposite, because what would have happened to her without him? And it seems that the rumors that were racing around about them weren't true. Only, it can't really be helped, Milliquet lodged a complaint…"

We were watching this empty café, this terrace with its decidedly oversized tables that were the wrong color green; we were watching Milliquet wander around. And that Saturday we also see that a storm is gathering (it hit during the party). The men spoke a little in front of the doors where they were pushing a broom back and forth, as usual, while, if they had girls, the girls were getting ready, and if they had boys, the boys were doing the same. These are parties that last more or less officially from Saturday to Monday evening; so, in terms of taking care of the animals, the sons make arrangements with their fathers; and in terms of housekeeping, the girls work something out with their mothers. Then they can go into their rooms and make themselves pretty, having first gone to the fountain for a full bucket of water for their bath. And the boys take their razors and some soap powder out of a drawer. The heavy weather made it feel good to put aside one's dirty clothes in exchange for clean ones, a white shirt; or one of those barely-there muslin dresses with no blouse (or as little blouse as possible). We put on a white or pink dress, a muslin or light silk dress. So the girls were getting themselves ready; the boys were getting themselves ready.

And so was this other one getting himself ready, but without anyone aware of the fact. Behind the sheds, at the end of the passage, having locked his door, he packed up a first bag. It's Saturday night; he takes a cloth bag and fills it to the brim, then he closes it with a double knot. He goes to place it in a corner. The other bag, he keeps it close to him: it's a bag we know well, and recognize easily because the waxed cloth covering which buttons along the side hides nothing of its shape. This bag he keeps close at hand, in order to slip the strap over his body when the time comes. He had returned all the different shoes he'd been given to repair: the ones remaining were lined up on their plank. Just then the Gavillet musicians were starting to be heard. Over the rooftops, we saw the woods up high on the other side of the ravine, and it was exactly at the tip of the woods where the sawtooth line of pine trees began to tremble along a strip of blue sky. We didn't notice the hunchback go out with his two bags. Now he had three humps. It was easy to see his three humps; it wasn't dark enough yet not to see them. There wasn't enough space for all three on his back so they stuck out on each side of his body, one to the right, the other to the left: the third couldn't move about. He went up the little street, because this isn't where we belong. He passed near the train station. All he had to do then was walk along the train tracks and follow the big road, which begins to descend, something which forces a series of hairpin turns, but there the hunchback steps off the road. He turned to the left. Here we were very close to the music; there was nothing more between it and us except the distance running flat between one side of the ravine and the other: the music was turning behind his humps, it was dancing along his sides; it made him go faster, even if he was sliding along the grass. We saw the viaduct move like it was covered in smoke. The hunchback heads for the side of the viaduct, there where the arches are pushed farther and farther into the hillside, and which cuts it obliquely, becoming lower and lower; he went toward the lowest of the arches, beneath which there is just enough space to slide along. He enters the space. He went back out. It's done.

Because now he only had two humps; he was just as he always was when Décosterd went to get him; he no longer had his bag but only his two usual loads, like when it was his job (and it was his job again this evening – this Saturday) to go to Rouge's; only he saw that today he was going to be late, and so he speeds up his steps. In fact, Décosterd is waiting for him. As he arrives in the little street, he saw that Décosterd is there and must have been there for quite some time, because Décosterd said to him, "Where are you coming from? Luckily, you're here. I was about to go back alone and what would Rouge have said?" The hunchback followed Décosterd.

Décosterd was saying, "It's understood. We'll unhook the

boat... And you, you bring Miss Juliette to the party. The boys know what they've got to do. And you've got nothing to be afraid of, because you'll be well-guarded on the road. Bolomey will make his rounds..."

The hunchback nodded.

That night, they watched a first storm. It happened as all four of them were seated in front of the house, and Rouge said to Urbain, "Louder."

It was because of the music from the Fleur-de-Lys that was carried down to us on a little wind along the Bourdonnette; it was making Rouge irritated, "Won't they ever be quiet? Louder, Mr. Urbain." They were seated on the bench. Suddenly, there was an abrupt change in the direction of the air, the wind began to blow from the southwest.

We saw the entire cavalry of waves jump into their saddles. We watched the horsemen come with their white flags.

The storm hung behind the mountains of the Savoy in a kind of curtain onto which the lightning made pink flashes; the cavalry began to gallop. We watched them—in the bottom of our bay, on our bench,—we watched them pass along the middle of the lake in long, straight lines and deep beneath the white flags they were bearing; in deep rows furrowed with lightning, then left again alone to the night.

The wind lifted up the little stones to our right and hurled them at our cheeks with other objects, making a strange noise like paper, or dry sticks, a sheet of aluminum, we weren't sure what, then it was the topside of a box. It wasn't raining.

Rouge was saying, "The storm won't be for us."

We see his face and his entire mustache, then that he brings his pipe to his mouth.

We see his entire face with its cotton ball mustache beneath which he had the time to bring up the tube of his pipe and it had time to be raised; then his face disappears, he has no more face; but the storm was already moving away.

The hunchback left fairly early; it's this Saturday night; as usual, Décosterd went with him.

And Rouge waited until he left, then he said to Juliette, "So, your things?... Juliette, it's tomorrow night... Juliette, you won't forget?"

As the story goes, several stands had arrived at the Fleur-de-Lys, including one that was selling gingerbread, another selling ice creams, and a third selling all kinds of little souvenirs for both adults and children. First, we make the rounds of the stands. The gingerbread stand was draped in a red Hadrianopolis cloth. The ice cream vendor's was painted in fake marble. The wooden horse carrousel had been nothing but a green carriage with windows, beneath which a dog whimpered and with a white horse attached to a stake; now, two men in khaki shirts and American suspenders each carried one horse in their arms or both of them a white buggy with the neck of a swan; then there were also these paintings and on the front of the orchestrion four rows of copper pipes. It was shining, it was lovely to look at. The young people arrived early in the morning in order to be there when the dancing started, the older people would come later because it's a custom for the men to sleep late on Sundays, even as late as three o'clock. In the village, Milliquet had seen a few customers that morning, and there had even been more than usual, something which was a welcome surprise; but, alas, everyone had left before noon. Even though now it was close to three o'clock, the terrace remained empty, the café as well; and Milliquet, standing on the doorstep, in his Sunday clothes with a collar and a tie, sometimes facing the water where there wasn't even a hint of someone coming, sometimes facing the top of the street which he could see in its full length;—only nothing was there that didn't turn its back to him right away. People were coming out of their houses, but they were all heading toward the music and the promise of pleasure in the sound of the trombone, coming over the roofs from time to time with one or two of its notes. Until Chauvy heads in this direction, with his little cane, his bowler hat, his jacket; so Milliquet shouts to him, "Hey you, where you going?" But Chauvy raises his little cane.

"Hey now," Milliquet said, "hey now, you! Chauvy!"

But Chauvy can't hear anymore and Milliquet thrusts his hands deep into his pockets and shrugs his shoulders, until he saw Perrin come out from his house just opposite.

"Say, Perrin, I think you'd better hurry. It'll only be two or three more days, this affair…"

Perrin looks at him without understanding.

"Yes, two or three days at the most… And then we'll see who gets the upper hand, honest folk or cheats…"

The other understood, but didn't answer. He also walks up the street. And then (but this was something Milliquet so little expected that it was his turn not to understand right away) there came little Marguerite; she comes, she's made herself beautiful.

"I've come to ask you for permission to go to the party for a bit."

"Huh?"

Milliquet looked at the dress she'd put on, a pink muslin dress with a white sash, and she was wearing little black boots and a woven paper hat.

"You.... you're crazy!" He was just starting to find his words when she interrupted.

"Oh!" she said, "It's just that I must go... and since there's nothing to do here."

"What? You must... must, she says..."

Just then, we heard a door open; a voice comes down the stairs.

"Say now, you old fool, are you going to let yourself be cheated yet again... let yourself be cheated by this little girl? Grab her, I tell you, grab her arm. And then lock the door..."

But it was too late. Marguerite had already dashed off.

And Mrs. Milliquet comes down, bent in half, a hand on her back, her skirt sideways, dragging her feet in her slippers; she was yelling, "You're going to hold back her wages... you keep her things... she won't come back here again. You hear me, I'm the boss here... You, you're finished, you're a failure... go lie down, you old fool, that's the best thing for you to do."

The slam of the door. This is how things happen on this earth.

At one o'clock, the musicians had arrived. There were eight of them. It's the Gavillet band. It's the most beautiful and the best of the music from around here. They were wearing dark gray suits, black felt hats, black silk ties, white shirts with broad, turned-down collars; they first went to drink something in the bar. They drank standing at the counter, as they were in a hurry, and were each holding his instrument (carefully polished with *Brillant Belge*) under his arm. They go out. The bugle gave the order with a solo melody like at a military service. Then everything began to quake and quiver softly all the way to the village; it was quaking softly against the wood, it was quivering softly in everyone's hearts.

She had come, she had come all alone; she had come along the back paths. There were too many people around for anyone to notice her, especially between the dance numbers. She walked along the line of stands, looking for him everywhere without finding him. She stops, turns to the right, to the left: all she sees is a big hand go into a white iron trunk and come out with a puppet with two feathers on its head, a red one and a black one; then the hand stands it up with other puppets also having white sugar for their eyes, red sugar for their lips, an embroidered collar and frog fastenings. It seems people are speaking to her. Automobiles arrive. All the youth from another village arrive as well, all dressed up, and they've come on their bicycles, on bicycles now gray with dust but whose handlebars are decorated with flowers and garlands. This is how things happen on this earth. A girl is alone on this earth. People say hello to her, she hasn't heard. The ball has just begun. She goes to stand behind the plank wall adorned with sweet-smelling pine boughs; this is where the women and the children stand, and those who are too old to dance. We see the eight musicians on the stage, seated beside one another behind their music notebooks; behind their music they were puffing out their cheeks. She was watching without seeing anything or she was seeing only one thing: that he wasn't there, he still wasn't there. There was a great mass of backs, heads, hands held into the air, hands resting on white shoulders, on pink shoulders, hatless heads, heads with hats, faces with mustaches, faces without mustaches;—the dance ended. Emilie went to sit down near the exit door, where the couples, one after the other, walked past holding each other's arms. And Maurice isn't there. We are on this earth. The musicians had taken the mouthpieces off their instruments; they were blowing inside, then they were shaking the instruments to let the saliva fall out, beneath the flags, beneath the garlands. And you see that we've made ourselves beautiful. You think maybe we'll stay this way all week! It's a party, we've changed our dresses, we've changed our eyes, we've changed our faces; you see, we're wearing white gloves:—they've been brought by the men on their horses, but, me, what am I doing here? While the men lead them into the garden and get them a drink of lemon soda around the green-painted iron tables, on the folding chairs. Me, where am I going to go? A great shadow falls across the light on the white path which becomes gray, a shadow over the sun in the sky that now covers, on the grass, on the tables, there where everyone is drinking, there where everyone is having fun, there where everyone is laughing. The wooden horses were static and turning; the children blow silently into the paper trumpets. The crowd was pushing her again between the stands where the little men with their sugar eyes watch her beneath their feathers. Then she sees a cage set down on a folding table next to a car for a cripple. A legless man says, "Your future, Ladies and Gentlemen!" She sees a platter in front of the cage with many slips of colored paper, folded into squares.

"It's two cents," the man is saying. "Two cents for a turn."

This is how it goes, this is on earth.

"Your future, ladies and gentlemen; two cents, only two cents…"

On earth, one afternoon, this last Sunday;—she is only a poor little girl, which is why she gives her two coins.

We see the cage grow larger for your two coins. The cage comes to meet you, becomes enormous, everything around you does the same. Nothing but the cage and the end of a wand that she watches, that taps three times; then:

"Attention! Mr. Know-it-all, are you ready?"

The bird has come to sit on the perch behind the door of the cage. He isn't moving anymore. Again three taps. The wand goes forward, the wand opens the door. People are pushing behind Emilie to try to see what's happening and a little girl's voice says, "You see, Mommy, the little bird! Oh, he's so funny! Oh, what is he doing, Mommy? Why is he taking the papers like that with his beak?" Then a fat woman: "It sure looks like he knows something." And it's true, because he is still looking at Emilie, he is looking at her from the side with his little shiny round eye, then with a quick movement of his beak, he picked up one of the notes, it's a pink one, but it must not be the good one because he throws it into the air with an abrupt jerk of his head, then it's a white one. But this isn't the good one either.

"Won't he make up his mind?"

"Oh, these animals are clever!"

"Is this the one? No…"

Who is speaking? Where are they speaking? While the bird is now holding a gray paper in its beak and we saw that this one is finally the one because he hopped over and landed on his master's hand.

"Let's see, Mr. Know-it-all, is this the good one this time?"

The bird nods.

"You're sure you're not making a mistake?"

The bird nods.

"Well now, Mr. Know-it-all, you know what you've got to do now."

The bird comes to her, the bird bowed to her three times and the man says, "Miss, it's for you…"

Emilie holds out her hand.

"Ladies and gentlemen, who's next?"

And all around her everyone was curious, but she shoves the square of paper into her cotton glove, turns around and leaves.

The air is filled with music, noises, voices, the air is filled with things that shine, move, turn; there are too many things everywhere, she feels the paper against her skin, she doesn't dare yet, she leaves the path.

Now she is in the orchard, she is in the grass beneath the trees.

She saw that the cherry trees had already changed color without their cherries, but she saw in the apple and the pear trees a future promise of good fruit. My God! Maybe... Does a person know? Does a person ever know? She went beneath the low branches; when she closed her hand she felt the angles of the paper prick into her skin. We saw that one of the slanted roofs was shiny like it'd been polished with egg white while another was matt, colorless. It's like us, it's like me. Alas, a girl is only ever lit up on one side, no matter what we do. There is only ever one side of us that receives the light... one has to dare... maybe...

And there, behind a tree trunk, she slips the ends of her fingers to get the paper from her glove.

A tender heart...

We see there are four printed lines: this is the first of the four lines, they all rhyme, it's a poem. Each phrase begins with a capital letter. She reads the first line.

And then comes the rest, and the paper says:

A tender heart
Will wait in vain
A heart of stone
Success will gain

The hunchback arrived at Rouge's close to four o'clock; Décosterd had gone to get him as usual. Rouge had taken advantage of the time that Décosterd wasn't there and hadn't come back yet to call Juliette. Again, he speaks to her through the door of her room, through the pinewood panel with its veins and knots:

"Juliette, did you think to put your things together?"

There was no immediate response.

"Urbain is coming," Rouge said, "so I thought we should agree together once more before he gets here... Juliette."

She hadn't replied, but she did open the door and Rouge could see that all was ready.

He sees that on the bed is a bundle wrapped in cloth and closed with a strap; he sees it, he sees everything, at first he is surprised:

"Oh, you're not taking your suitcase? We'd have had room for it in the boat. It's practical, a boat, we could put all the furniture in it... well, maybe you're right."

He started again, "Anyway, we'll find what we need over there... not worth weighing ourselves down with luggage, especially if we're arriving in the middle of the night... I'll write a card immediately to Décosterd. All I need to do is hide the key; Décosterd knows where I hide it... and I'll tell him... what do you think if I tell him he can stay here while we're away?"

She still doesn't answer; he doesn't seem to notice:

"Anyway, I can always write him... the only thing that's worrying me..."

He turned toward the front door, he was still being very calm. "The only thing that's worrying me is that we're going to have a storm. The one from last night didn't finish itself out..."

He went forward to the front step. "Well," he said, "it

won't be long now. But anyway (and then he went back to it) the storm... you're not afraid of the storm, are you, Juliette? And you're not afraid of waves either? It's just that. I'll worry about the rest. Anyway, the boat is good. We repaired it for you, remember? And it's got your name on it... three short hours and we'll be there... you'll help me row, won't you... it's just that... Oh, Juliette!"

Then something stopped inside him, knotted up in the back of his throat, "We can tell... yes, we can really tell that... blood-relation..."

He had trouble speaking.

"When someone's related, as if we were... father and... Juliette..."

And then we see him move forward, but at the same time the sound of footsteps made him move backward; and he said quickly, "Close your door, Juliette. Hide your bundle..."

He was in front of the house when Décosterd and the hunchback arrived. Outside the house the sun was scorching as if someone was bringing a red hot poker toward your face, like the blacksmith making a joke, or to get the kids to run off away he shoves the hot iron at them that he's just pulled from the fire. If we turned around, we immediately felt the scorch of the sun at the edge of our collars; below the line it remained cool. Décosterd moved his head over his shoulder, gestured with his head in its everyday cap toward the lake bottom and, in the still air, he half closes his eye, without saying a word; so Rouge nods his head. Before the water, Décosterd was all black, while the water was like a sheet of tin-plated iron.

"Yes, yes," said Rouge. "Well, Mr. Urbain," he continues, "I think it's going to be too hot to stay outside... and, anyway, you've got some competition."

He makes a movement with his head backward and behind him.

"And they won't be stopping soon, because today's the big day... they've got permission from the police... until two o'clock in the morning, that makes for a while. And those guys over there, they can alternate with each other, the music, I mean. Sometimes there are two of them... And sometimes there are three of them. And well, you..."

He starts to laugh. Urbain set his accordion on the bench.

And, in fact, while they were speaking, the sky over by the Bourdonnette continued to raise itself up slowly, then fell again in little steps; it was white like cloth over the black hedge of pine trees. The lowest notes were the only ones that managed to come to us distinctly, more or less muted and more or less held long, sometimes lasting until a breath finished, sometimes pushed against each other in short bursts like soap bubbles. And no one anywhere, no one on the water, no one on the shoreline; no one beneath the white sky, nor at the quarry, nor on the cliff, nor among the water-worn stones that rubbed off the leather of your shoes, nor on this water a person couldn't look at without ruining his eyes.

And Rouge said, "Finally, today there's a chance we won't be bothered. Come on, Mr. Urbain, you've got to come into the kitchen. We'll be better here... and I've still got one or two bottles... it's now or never..."

We go inside. Rouge goes to get the bottles. He goes himself to lay them down in the water on the sand which he scoops out so that the water covers them entirely; it appeared he had nothing to fear for them today as the water was so still, beneath its tin cover. Rouge is in a good mood. Too bad if the wine isn't as fresh as chilled champagne. "What do you say, Décosterd? And you, Mr. Urbain?"

Then he calls, "Hey, Juliette!"

While the three of them sit down, one last time around the Battle of the Bourget, in the kitchen; and we hear the party, while the marine rifleman raises his boarding axe. We hear the party, a shell explodes, making a black-rimmed white circle in one part of the waxed cloth where the weft is visible. The sky over the lake was becoming ever more impenetrable.

She came in just then or a bit after; she came out of her room just then, or a little later. And, as she'd just opened her door and hadn't yet shut it, suddenly, in the great stillness of the air, a gust of wind came in and held aloft a woodchip halfway between the ceiling and the floor, while the door rattled.

It was a chip from the *Coquette*, from when we'd resanded it and before we changed its name; a little bit of green could still be seen, a little bit of the oil paint was still caught in its fibers.

My bottles!

Rouge runs outside. It was just as she'd come in. She lets go of the door that closes by itself with a slam; Rouge had just enough time to grab the bottles by their neck. The lake had begun to brew (this is how we call it), at the same time it had darkened, and its lovely shine was like a metal turning rusty. The lake was brewing, meaning that everywhere it was raising itself up, but the waves had no direction, they were rising and falling in one place, like water being heated on a fire. Rouge quickly grabs the bottles by their necks, he came back with the bottles; he placed them on the table, but again the wind had stopped; Rouge wipes his sleeve across his forehead. He'd taken his knife from his pocket, and while shoving the bottle opener into the cork, the bottle between his knees, he'd turned to Juliette:

"Well, what do you say, Juliette?"

He was in a good mood, and gay.

"It's nearly as hot as those countries where you come from."

"Oh, not quite."

"Not yet? It'll come…"

Then he says, "In any case, this is weather that makes you thirsty, but you see that here we've got what a person needs to cure a thirst, while you, over there, you've got no wine… there isn't any wine in those countries…"

She shook her head. And, now, outside it was like when a lot of people are speaking at once, like when a fairground is filled with men in discussion; we could no longer hear the music. There was only the sound of the cork.

Rouge filled the glasses.

He was saying, "It's our little wine, wine we've made… and it's not so bad as all that, not bad to look at, not so bad to the taste…"

He was saying, bringing the glass to his nose, "Oh, she doesn't know about it, but you, Mr. Urbain, because, in your country, people know their wine…"

He was saying, "Cheers! …Cheers! Juliette!… Cheers, Mr. Urbain… and to you, my old friend Décosterd."

We remember that just then, she (Juliette) was seated on the table, and Rouge was near her on the bench.

The hunchback was seated a little further away, against the wall, on a chair.

Again a gust of wind came in, and the Battle of the Bourget was lifted up at one corner and flipped upside down, showing its fuzzy underside. Several minutes passed. Rouge was still speaking, he had to raise his voice louder and louder. That afternoon the accordion remained in its waxed cloth case. The girl, she holds her knee in her hands, in such a way that her little foot stuck out from her leg, the ankle so slender one could encircle it with one's fingers; she was wearing silk stockings (they were stockings she had found in the package Rouge had brought back from the city) — and far away, meaning off to the southwest, we hear a first roll of thunder. Oh! This time it wouldn't be long (which we could also see by the complete change of the light); so you have to imagine that the door had stayed open. And Décosterd was no longer there. You have to imagine how Rouge goes to this door and how he blocks about two-thirds of the view, and we saw running on Rouge's shoulders the first white crests moving regularly from west to east. Rouge goes to the doorstep, then goes forward a little further onto the sand; we see him turn his head. He turns his head suddenly toward the cliff; someone was calling him.

He yelled, "What is it?"

The hunchback looked at Juliette; she jumped down from the table.

She was standing up on both feet, then it is her turn to go out of the house where she sees Rouge who has headed toward where the calling was coming from. It was Décosterd calling him. Over where he's standing, Décosterd raises one of his arms, then both. Rouge hurries even more.

The hunchback hadn't moved. The girl, she'd moved forward to just about halfway between the house and the water; once there, she stops in the wind that rolls her skirt around her legs like the string of a whip around a spinning top. She sees Rouge about to meet Décosterd. Again, Décosterd is making signs with his arms. Rouge was listening. Then we saw him shrug his shoulders. Suddenly, Rouge turned around, he saw Juliette. He hesitated just a moment, then he quickly turned around.

Now he is the one calling. "Juliette, hey, Juliette!"

So he came straight toward her, while she goes to meet him, because we can no longer hear each other unless standing close.

"Juliette, one of the boats has come undone: it's yours... the one we needed..."

So she says, "Can't I go with you?"

"Out of the question..."

And, as if the request reassured him, "We'll go after it quickly, Décosterd and me, before the waves chase it out too far... Listen, Juliette, we won't be gone long... and there's Mr. Urbain here... all you need to do is close the door."

He turned his back to her, he walked away quickly, then, turning one last time, he said, "Juliette! You understand? Close and lock the door."

As for the boys, they had set themselves up in different places from which we could best see her coming. Bolomey was standing at the top of the cliff, Maurice was on the other side of the ravine near the quarry, Alexis had positioned himself a little ways in front of the dance floor (and where the two mortars were as well). The three of them had gotten together, then had asked some of their friends to help; and the friends had said, "Of course she should come... will she be wearing her costume? Oh, what a party it's going to be! And for the mortars, we're agreed. It's been a while we haven't used them. It's the perfect time... Yes, we'll hide them in the bushes." They had quickly agreed on all points and we'd explained to them that we'd found a way that Rouge was obliged to let her come and Décosterd was taking care of it... Everything had been set up with the greatest care by the three of them, Alexis, Bolomey and Maurice; now they were at their posts, while the party was in full swing. We weren't worried about the storm, especially because the dance floor was covered. Only women who'd come with children, mothers, some older women, had decided it best to head home. And, while this was happening, Bolomey, up on the cliff, had seen Décosterd call Rouge, then seen that Rouge was coming, then that they'd gone together into the second of the boats, the first had just this second been hit on the side by the waves just above the opening of the Bourdonnette. While the women on the road were pushing their little carriages or holding hands with the children old enough to walk, Bolomey slides down the ravine to go join up with Maurice below the quarry. And Maurice was watching the spot where, between two bushes, the road opens up from off the ravine. Bolomey was coming down, then Bolomey meets up with Maurice, then the two of them join Alexis.

It was just in front of the dance floor, a little below it, and an entire row of hedges provided a hiding place for us. Behind the shrubs were the two mortars. They waited there, the three of them. We were facing the road that came straight toward us, along the river between the alders, and then between two wide banks beneath the sky which we could see to the southwest. And, there, it becomes another color; and a dark blue like glazed pottery made it look like a hillside that rises always more steeply, then begins to rise forward into an overhang: at the same time the wind rises, at the same time the light changes...

And the girl also changed the light, the light around her becomes all white. There was this great black sky, but everything around her was lit up (or she was the one lighting it). They were watching her come, and she was still in the bottom of the valley, still fairly far away; she was red against the night. Behind her was the hunchback, the hunchback was also in the shadow. He was at the limit of the darkness where we see the pine trees leaning off together in one large group. He was holding his instrument in front of him, tilting his head to the side, pulling on the bellows; then he presses his two hands upon them, making it twist. He has two humps; we can only see one, the one in front of him. He is just in the line of the shadow creating the night; every time he leaves it, the line comes farther forward. And farther forward is the girl; and there on her is two times the light because she calls it to her, and adds to it at the same time; she is lit up and she lights up. And now it seems nothing is in proportion and she is no longer her usual size; the wind has taken her, the wind pushes her, she is lifted up; she stands on one foot, then on the other; she turns, she turns again, all the light turns with her;—and the men up above, only the three men see her approaching, they see that it will be too late; so Alexis yells, "Hey! Ready?... Fire!"

We see two flames as long as canes, two white flames in the white day. Fire! Fire! Two flames, each a full meter long; then the two lines of short grass tumble down the hillside, hit against one another.

We see the hunchback has stopped.

The accordion has quieted, we can no longer hear the accordion; what we hear is a first echo in the ravine make its noise like a sailcloth stretching out, like when the wind smacks hard into the great sail. And the sound of the second echo. Then the third. Like a sailcloth taking on water or like when the wind slackens. The music from the party quieted behind them; the eight musicians on the bandstand dropped their instruments from their mouths, their cheeks still puffed with air that wasn't used; and now this is truly where she belongs, because everyone is coming. She is still shining with her red shawl, she is shining with her naked arms, she shined with her teeth; —everyone is coming, Maurice, Bolomey, Alexis; we see Chauvy coming, we see little Marguerite coming; they're holding paper roses, they stand in a line, they give her the roses. She slides along before us, while the hunchback follows her. Again, he leaned his head to the side; his fingers raced along the keys...

Over on the cliff, no one had seen the Savoyard. The girl had stepped onto the dance floor, passing beneath a garland holding a sign covered in words of welcome; —him, over there, even Bolomey hadn't been able to detect him. She has just stepped onto the dance floor, we moved out of her way, we were standing in a circle; —and the Savoyard was sniggering over there beneath his little oak tree with its hanging branches, happy to see that Bolomey hadn't seen him even though he was only a few steps away. We told Gavillet he could let his musicians rest, because we were saying to the hunchback at the same time: "And now it'll be your turn..." And we were also saying, "Time to turn the lights on," because it was so dark now. She was now beneath the roof of the dance floor, but this night having come early was a problem; the boys yell, "Go on and tell the inn to give us some electricity," — the man over on the cliff sniggers. He sees directly below him how the battle has started, the two men are there in the boat and the boat moves toward him against the movement of the waves. He feels in his pocket if the box of matches is still there, if the two boxes that he took, just to be sure, are still there; they're there. There is plenty of time. And maybe the men in their boat won't be done as quickly as they'd believed; all the better. He watches how they fight and struggle against the waves. Ravinet was looking at Rouge, he was looking at Décosterd. The boat was moving to the side, while they were showing you their full selves including their feet planted flat onto the boards of the boat bottom. They were rising quickly, leaning toward you, then they made it over the crest of the wave; then suddenly their legs were gone, and their bodies, and their arms, finally their heads: they had gone down the other side. There was nothing left to do, the boat was sunk. No. We see it rise up again, surging with the rising wave; we see the two men turn themselves around with the oars, with all their might, trying to grab it... Oh!... he sneers. Well, they'll have enough to keep them busy even just to get themselves back in to shore! We've got time, we've got plenty of time! ... And now the eight musicians have gotten down off the bandstand behind Gavillet who'd said, "Don't mind, do we..." even if his pride was a little hurt, but he hid this and he was saying, "We've been playing for two hours straight." We said to him, "There's some wine waiting for you." The musicians go behind the paper roses and down the steps (it's more like a ladder) of the bandstand, and this was while Ravinet over on the cliff was going down the other steps, even steeper still, sandstone steps behind tufts of sweet clover, high stalks of soapwort, and amidst the low shrubs to which he holds onto over the difficult parts of the path; then he feels that he still has a box of matches in the pocket of his vest; that makes three in all; he's taken his precautions. And now we'll see exactly who I am. Ravinet... Cyprien Ravinet, from Saint-Dolloires. And we'll see if they'll make fun of me anymore. He finds the door to Rouge's house wide open. The wind going in freely, the same for the lightning and the first rolls of thunder. He goes in. When one cannot have, one destroys. At least they will see that I've been here; I'll leave my signature. He enters with the wind, with the pink and yellow lightning, while we can see that the waxed oilcloth has already been pushed by the wind into a corner. The stone floor is all covered with debris twisting about the table legs: wood chips, pieces of paper, dry leaves, cork floaters: all this kept spinning around, while he grabs a chair and throws it hard against the hanging oil lamp that tumbles down, spraying the walls. What remains of the liquid spreads across the table and from there runs onto the ground. He watches, pleased. He goes to the cupboard, he finds the jug of gasoline; he checks that the jug is full. He knocks his shoulder against this other door that is closed and laughs again, because the door jumps on the first hit. Here, we are in her space. The big mirror that had her so often will have her no more: one thing gained. When one cannot have, one destroys. Now he picks up one of the new and white-painted chairs that are there... we were saying to the musicians, "Go have a drink.... you can see, we've laid it all out for you, and there's something to eat, if you're hungry, there is bread and cheese";—but a star is made in the glass and his view of us vanishes. Crash against the mirror, and crash on the table: it's a lightly built object; it breaks in half. He poured gasoline over it, he pours over the bed; he throws all he can find on the bed along with her things, then he goes to the shed. The shed is made of wood. It is filled with the hanging nets: well, they're all dry and have been for awhile now, they've had plenty of time to dry these last fifteen days, three weeks they haven't been used: newspapers, gasoline, a match... here it goes. Luckily, we've got three boxes of matches. He goes back into her room, he puts these newspapers under the bed. He stacks the chairs, he strikes a match. He passes into the kitchen; there, he throws the waxed cloth onto the bench, and atop the straw-backed chairs. His last plan is to go into Rouge's room, but a great flame with a hot tip rose up between him and the door: he had just enough time to jump backward.

"And well, for the rest of us," we were saying, "we invited her mostly for a little amusement and a little variety; because we were thinking to ask the hunchback to play, and, and it seems she dances; we didn't know anything else. Gavillet wasn't very happy, but he wasn't showing it. He went down off the bandstand with his musicians. The girl, they had mussed her hair with a crown they'd wanted to put on her head. We see her hair is filled with little bits of moss, and we're laughing and they hand her a paper rose, then we see that she loses her shawl. Now she was standing in the middle of the dance platform: night had come even before six o'clock, in the middle of August, just like one of the darkest nights of winter. We could only still see her shoulders and her arms, once the shawl had fallen, but we pick it up for her. She takes the rose. 'The lights! The lights! Hey, over there, the lights!' because the switches were inside the inn… she slid the paper rose into her hair behind her ear… 'The lights!' A boom of thunder. We could no longer see, we could no longer hear one another. We made a loudspeaker with both hands… 'The lights! Hey…!' We were pushing toward her. And the thunder kept booming. The flashes of lightning were bright despite the lamps; then everything went black while the boom hit against our faces, behind our heads, against our shoulders. We couldn't tell where we were at. And as for me, I pushed further, but I was taken behind the first row, and between the first row and the second; so we couldn't see the hunchback, because he must have been seated. We couldn't see him; not a tall man even when standing, he was so short and now he was entirely hidden on his bench by people standing before him. And the girl, she could be seen between people's heads. We see her in snatches. She is given to you, she is taken away. A flash of lightning; then it seemed that the roof of the dance platform came down; the girl, she can be seen between people's heads, then she can no longer be seen. As people tell it now, just then the hunchback doffed his hat and placed it beside him; he gestured to it, he wasn't yet playing. He seemed to be waiting. It was those in the first row who understood first, having been able to see the whole thing. They understood, they were laughing. The girl, she seemed to be waiting as well, then she also gestures to the hat: and so a first coin falls into the hat. But the people in the other rows, having now understood, yelled, 'And what about us?' They got their money ready, they couldn't reach the hat. They held their coins in their hands, but they had to stand up on the tips of their toes, the hat was placed too low. So they yell, 'Pass it to us!' We were having fun. We were yelling, 'Pass the hat!' It seems the accordion began to play; we couldn't hear it. She began to go around the circle, while we were continuing to push toward her, and at the same time we split away from her when she moved toward you; in this way some were going forward, others were going backward. She was holding her arms out; bits of moss were still hanging in her hair. We were throwing one franc coins, two franc coins at her. Suddenly, a crack of lightning. Another crack. Everyone was digging in their pockets. But now the lights are flickering and weakening in the bulbs, inside which we can see the filaments; and now... now we are looking at the lake, someone turns around... and over there, amidst the flashes of lightning is one flash that held steady. In the dip of the valley, there was one that didn't want to go out. It remains fixed at the base of the sky; we heard the fire bell ring out..."

Some ran to the village to get the fire pump wagon; others took the path that descends along the Bourdonnette. Those on the path saw it lit up in front of them by a flash of lightning; then the ground was taken away so they were placing their steps into a void. Then the ground was lit again; they move faster, but they slip, they fall forward. They were no longer feeling the rain except for the water that ran along their sides and when they opened their mouths, they get a full mouthful. They slide, they fall forward, smashing against the night that has returned across the path as if there was a mudslide on the hill, but they call to one another or they hold hands; and, at the same time, behind the curtains of water was this great steady flame that made shine the strings of water and which they had only to fix their eyes upon and their bodies moved forward as if pulled by a long rope. They arrive at the ravine, they tumble about in the bushes. And they spill out finally onto the shoreline, while we could still hear the fire bell ringing, between two booms of thunder. The pump hadn't yet arrived; and anyway they saw that they had arrived too late.

And, in fact, when the fire wagon finally arrived, they didn't even get it working, even though there was plenty of water. There was already nothing left of the shed; as for the rest of the building, only the four brick walls were still standing and from a pile of fallen wooden beams a black smoke was rising, replacing the light of the flames. We were arriving from everywhere now, but there was nothing to do: we could only watch. And those who came from the village like those who came from the Fleur-de-Lys just stood there, without moving (the wind had lost much of its power, the waves too, and the thunder was moving away).

We were now in the gray air, on a gray water, in a fine gray rain; and amidst all this was the black smoke. They were standing there, they were standing around all that remained of the buildings; at first they said nothing, then we hear Milliquet's voice:

"This is the way it had to end!"

He had arrived behind the pump; he speaks loudly and is one of the first to speak. He had his hands in his pockets, he had a cloth bag on his head that gave him a pointed cap.

"And Rouge, where is he? Where's the girl?"

This is when Rouge appeared, but not the girl. Rouge appeared but she wasn't with him.

He was with Décosterd; the two men had just gotten back to shore. Their whole bodies dripped with water, their hair plastered to their foreheads, no hats, trousers stuck to their thighs; then they are standing there in the fine rain, and Rouge went forward and Décosterd followed him.

Rouge didn't seem to understand. Rouge was saying nothing, neither was Décosterd. It's Milliquet who starts again, "Oh, so there you are, you; And so what? Are you surprised?"

Everyone was quiet.

"No, I see that you're not surprised; only, *her*, where've you put her?"

Rouge didn't answer.

"Oh, well that's the top! So…you old fox, you let her get away?"

We saw Rouge lower his head. First he looks at Milliquet like he might jump on him; then his arms fall down next to his body. Something unknots in his neck, his head falls forward.

"It seems that she wasn't so happy with you, and this…"

Milliquet sneers, "Ok, that's good, now I'm avenged."

We had surrounded Rouge, because first we were afraid he would do something bad; we saw quickly that he wasn't even thinking of it.

We saw quickly that even if he'd thought of it he wouldn't have had the strength; and this is when that other voice came, this other voice rising over the water, fighting hard against the noise.

"Hey over there! Hey, old man…"

Someone was laughing on the waves; they were already much smaller and less powerful.

"Hey old man! Recognize me?"

It was the Savoyard. He had waited for Rouge to get to land; he had taken his boat.

And we understand one last thing that he yells: "In the mail… I'll send it back to you in the mail…"

A burst of laughter; Rouge doesn't move. It seems he will never move again and he'll stay standing there until the end of the world, while the rest of us grew quiet; we were standing in a circle around the smoking wooden beams.

The smoke from the beams had been black; now it was white.

And is she still here, still for a little while?

There were only a few who had stayed on the dance floor: Maurice, Alexis, Bolomey, little Marguerite, Chauvy; everyone else who'd been watching had run to the fire or gone for shelter in the inn. The electricity had gone out completely. Here, we were in the wind, in the lightning, in the thunder, and the thunder was continually growling. At the very most, every few moments and at great intervals, a note or two or even a chord came to you, then we hear nothing. We can no longer see the hunchback; we can no longer see Juliette. The night falls upon your head and around your shoulders like a photographer's black hood; then she appears, she is pink; she has gotten up onto a table. We see her, we no longer see her. There are only five or six of us. And so Alexis thought that it was definitely time, he leans toward Maurice, Maurice isn't there. He looks for him, holding his hand out but doesn't find him. Then Maurice is there again; Alexis has time to reach for his shoulder, he puts his hand on the shoulder, just when Maurice disappears again.

"Listen, Maurice, you've got to tell her it's time to get going, it's now, the storm is going to pass... it's time to take her, Maurice, before everyone comes back..."

But Maurice doesn't seem to hear, he is watching. She is there, she is no longer there.

"Maurice!"

Maurice doesn't answer, he hasn't moved. The wind comes, it slaps beneath the roof structure. The night grows longer, the flashes of lightning less frequent; they are now over the roof. Night—no, because she is there, she is there again; she holds her two arms up, the rose falls from her ear.

"Maurice!"

Then we hear a few shrill little notes that seem to grow distant, then come back, grow distant again; and where is he, the hunchback? We can't see him, nor his instrument, nor where the sound is coming from, because he's moved;—but she was raised up again into the air. The lightning paints her, she raises her arms. She raises her arms again; then she has no arms, then she has no body, then she is no more; and a last clap of thunder made it so everything ceased to exist; she ceased to exist as well, and, when the lightning came again, she was no longer there...

"Go quickly, Maurice, no one will see us... hurry!"

But Alexis stopped suddenly.

A little gray light had begun to slide itself between the wooden beams beneath the garlands; we see the garlands, and look at that, it's true, we're on the dance floor. We see between the floor and the ceiling all the things that are coming back to their places: the wet grass, the trees, their trunks; vaguely, not yet well-defined, like at the dawn of the world. It's as if the world is coming into existence and it isn't the same as before. Maurice then looks around him slowly, astonished, then he looks for her, for Juliette; he sees that she is in fact no longer there. We see the bench where the hunchback was seated, he is no longer there. And we see the table where she had been (or was it a dream we had, because she is no longer on the table). Not next to it, not anywhere. And Maurice looks, then he takes off running.

"Maurice, where're you going, hey, Maurice..."

He doesn't hear. He is in the fine gray rain which is hanging everywhere between you and the sky. There is fog, the trees are dripping. He goes toward the road; he gets to the road, he doesn't see her on the road. It's just that we can't see more than fifteen meters ahead, but maybe we've gone in the wrong direction, and now the fire bell has quieted, the wind has also stopped, the now far away thunder can barely be heard. And what a strange silence there is all around! And there amidst the dripping of the trees, while he turns around, because it's as if we've come up behind him; —and, in fact, someone has come, but it isn't the one he is looking for...

He shook his head.

We continue to call out to Maurice from beneath the dance platform, where now the boys are whistling as loud as they can with their fingers, not being able to see him, not able to be seen by him;—and her, he's seen her perfectly, little Emilie, he wasn't able not to see her because she came so close, her dress sodden against her shoulders, her large straw hat with the brim drooping down against the sides of her face.

He wasn't able not to hear her, "Maurice, it's me..."

She lowers her head; she stands there, hands together; over her skirt she holds her little brown hands that are soaking wet; but she isn't the one he's looking for.

She waits, she waits some more; we have turned our back to her.

And the footsteps move away, move always further away.

Ω

CPSIA information can be obtained at www.ICGtesting.com
Printed in the USA
BVOW08s0211160716

455405BV00002B/46/P